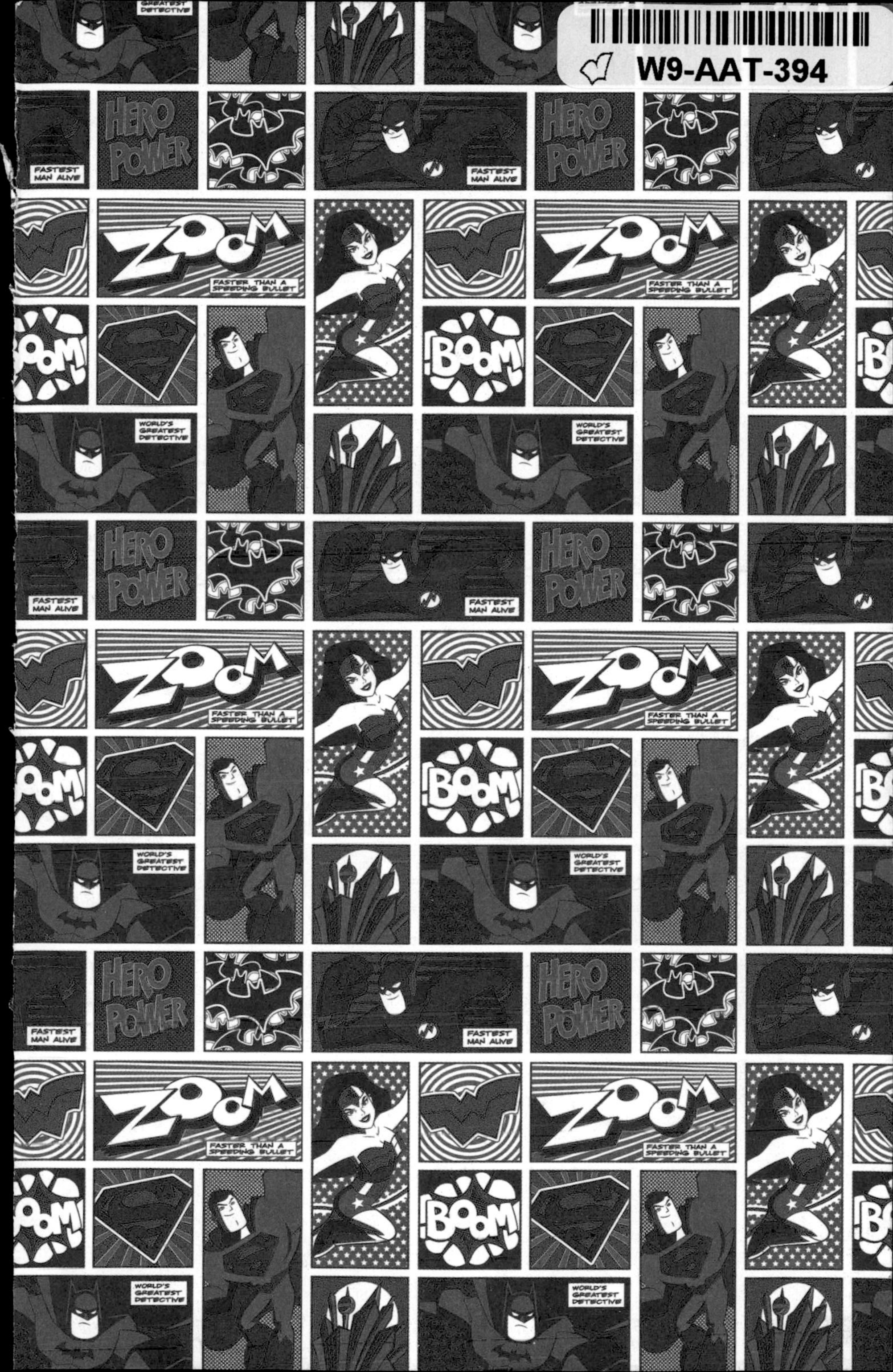
HERO POWER
FASTEST MAN ALIVE
ZOOM
FASTER THAN A SPEEDING BULLET
BOOM
WORLD'S GREATEST DETECTIVE

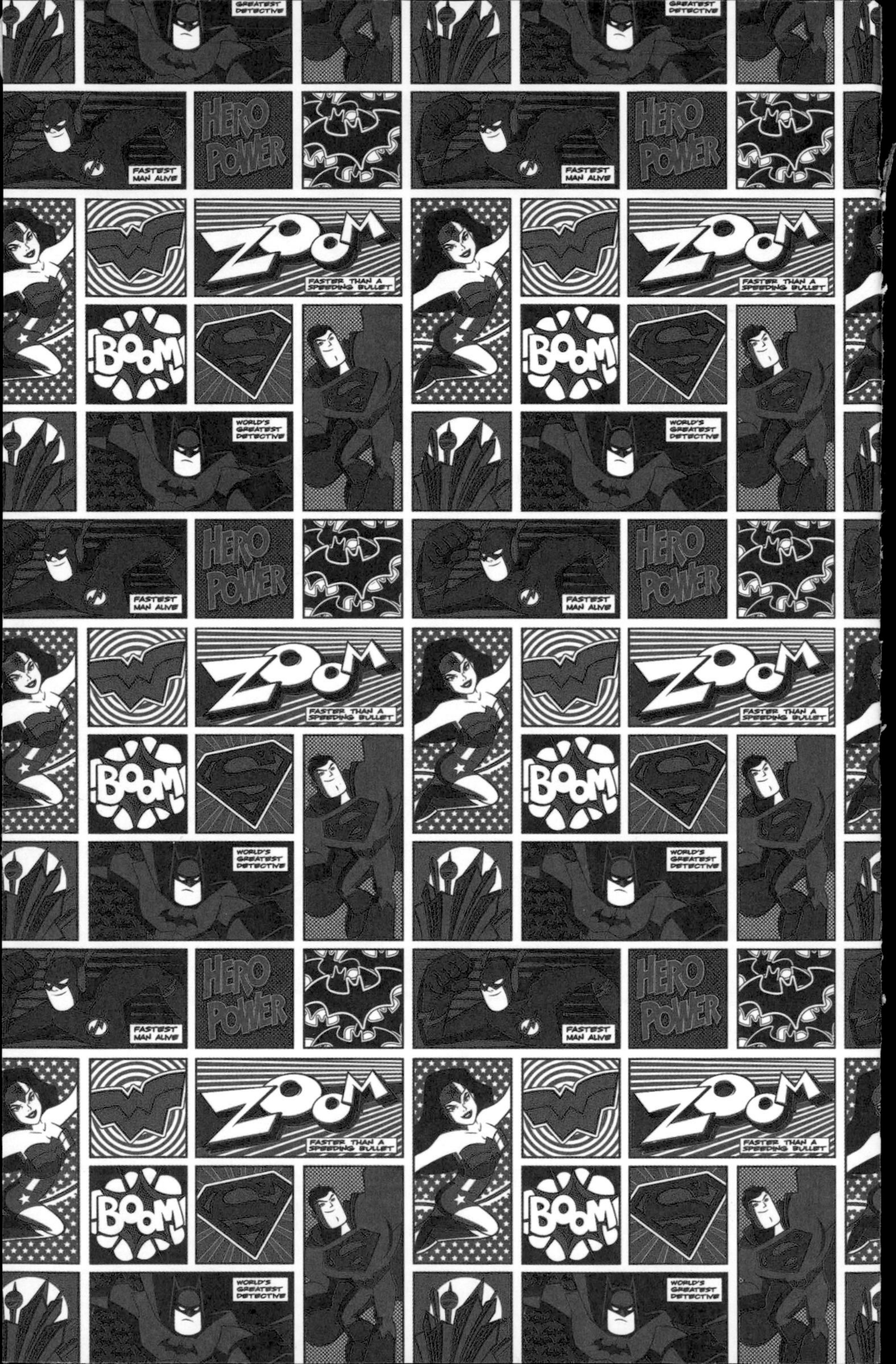
WORLD'S GREATEST DETECTIVE
HERO POWER
FASTEST MAN ALIVE
ZOOM
FASTER THAN A SPEEDING BULLET
BOOM!

DC SUPER FRIENDS™

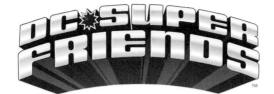

HOW TO BE A HERO

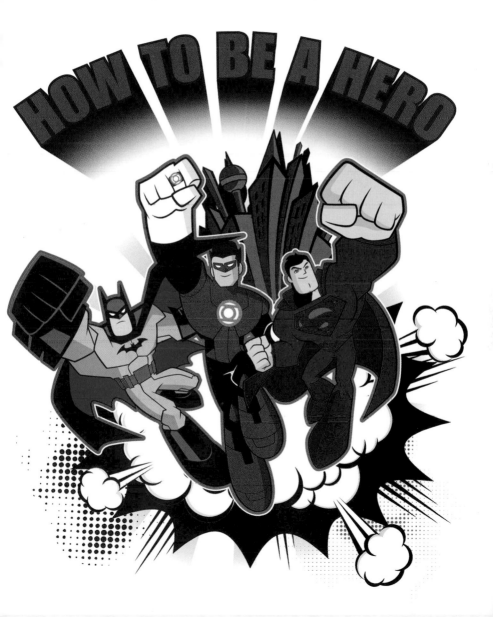

For Isaiah Bryant

—C.B.C.

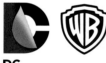

DC COMICS™

RHUS36460

 Published in the United States by Random House Children's Books, a division of Penguin Random House LLC, 1745 Broadway, New York, NY 10019, and in Canada by Penguin Random House Canada Limited, Toronto. Random House and the colophon are registered trademarks of Penguin Random House LLC.

randomhousekids.com

ISBN 978-1-101-93958-1 (trade) — ISBN 978-1-101-93959-8 (ebook)

Printed in the United States of America 10 9 8 7 6 5 4 3 2 1

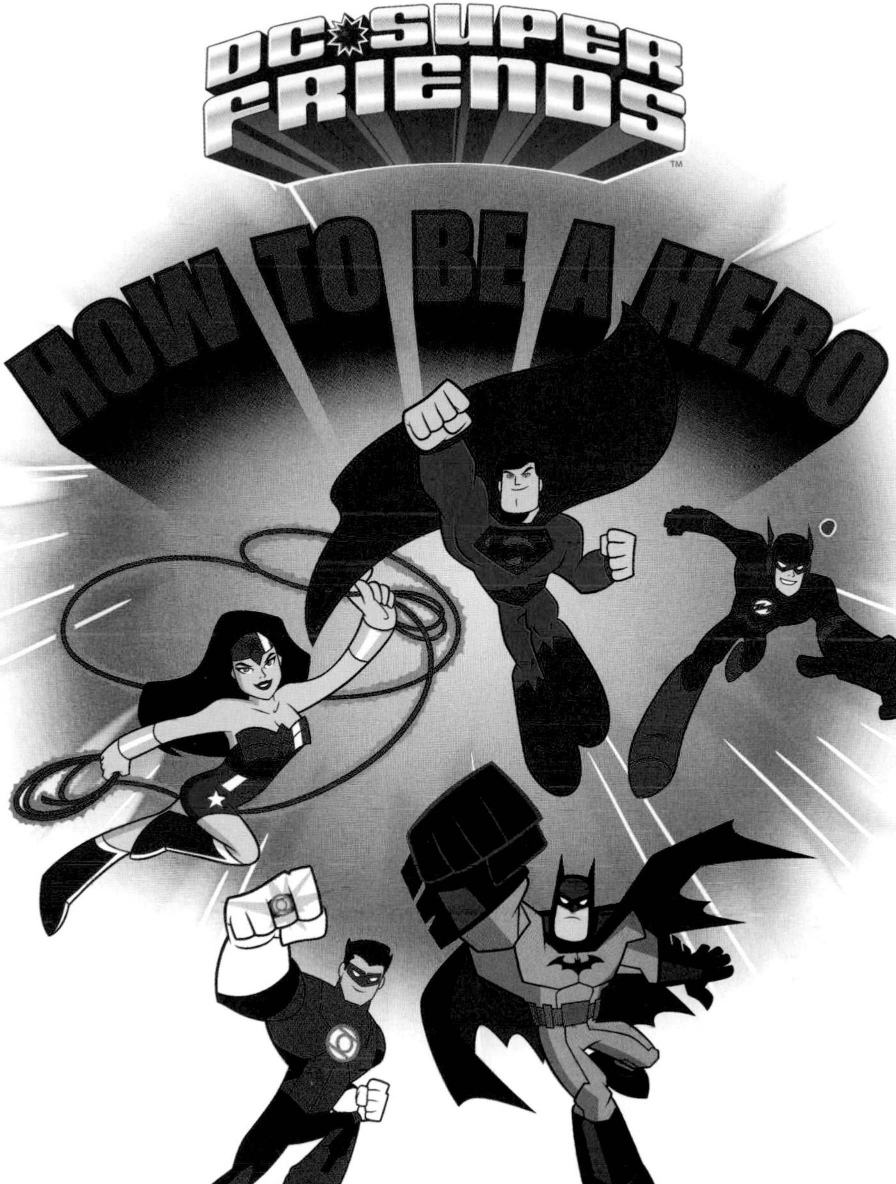
DC SUPER FRIENDS
HOW TO BE A HERO

By Courtney Carbone

Additional illustrations by Erik Doesher

Random House New York

CONTENTS

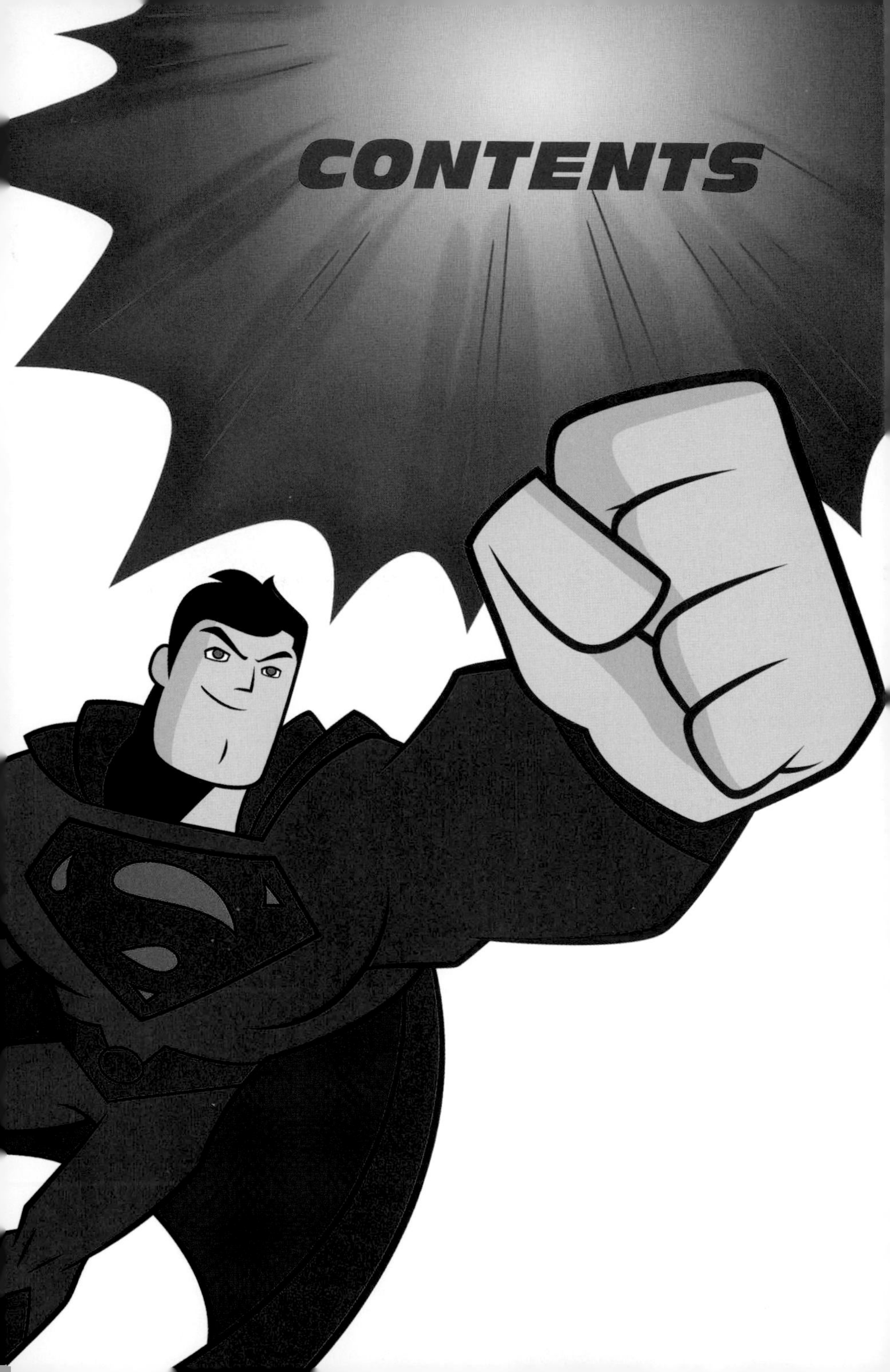

Introduction

Do you want to know what it takes to be a super hero like Superman, Wonder Woman, Batman, Green Lantern, and the other DC Super Friends?

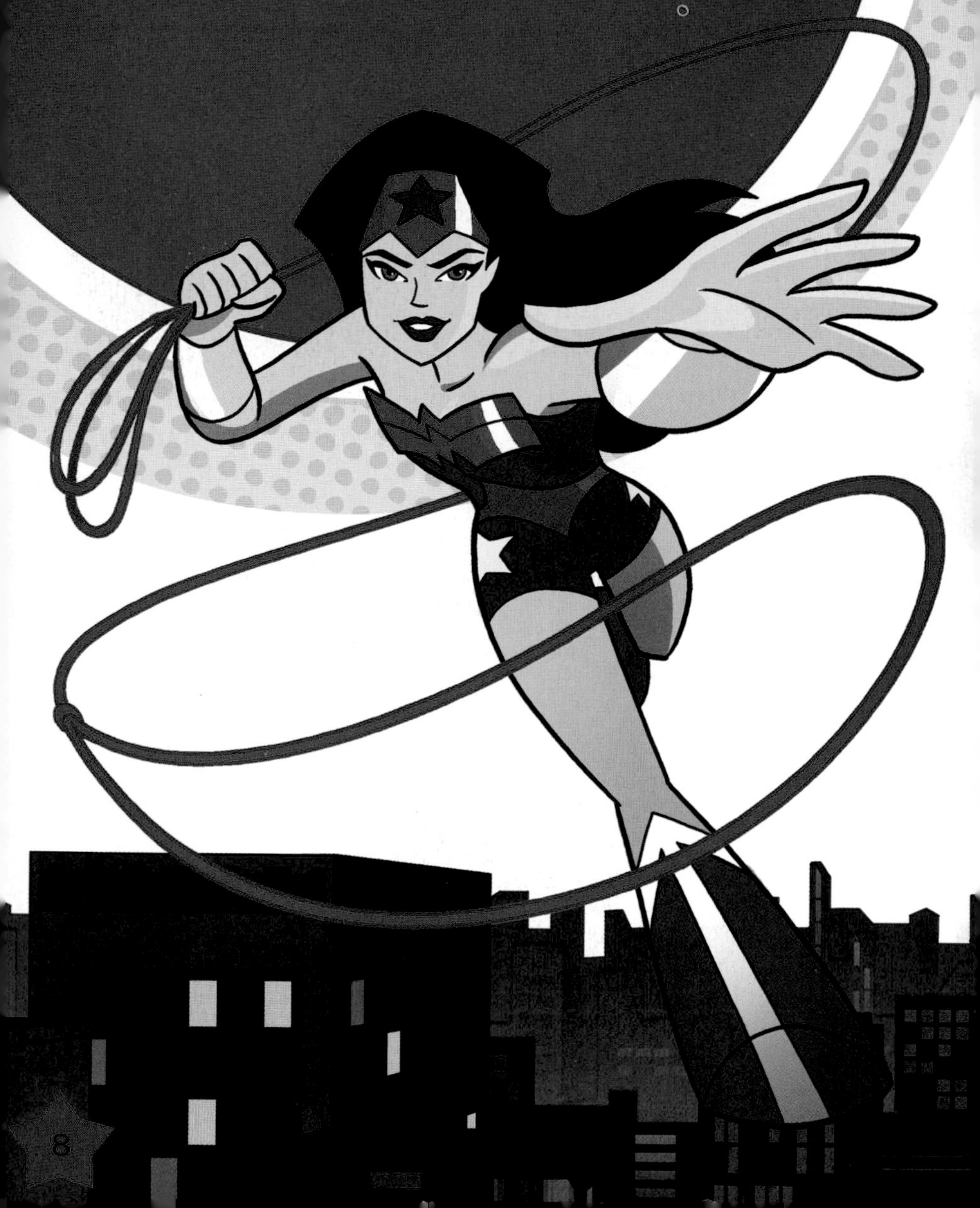

This book will serve as your manual for becoming a hero.

You'll learn how to choose your hero identity, create an iconic costume, and develop your superpowers to reach maximum hero potential.

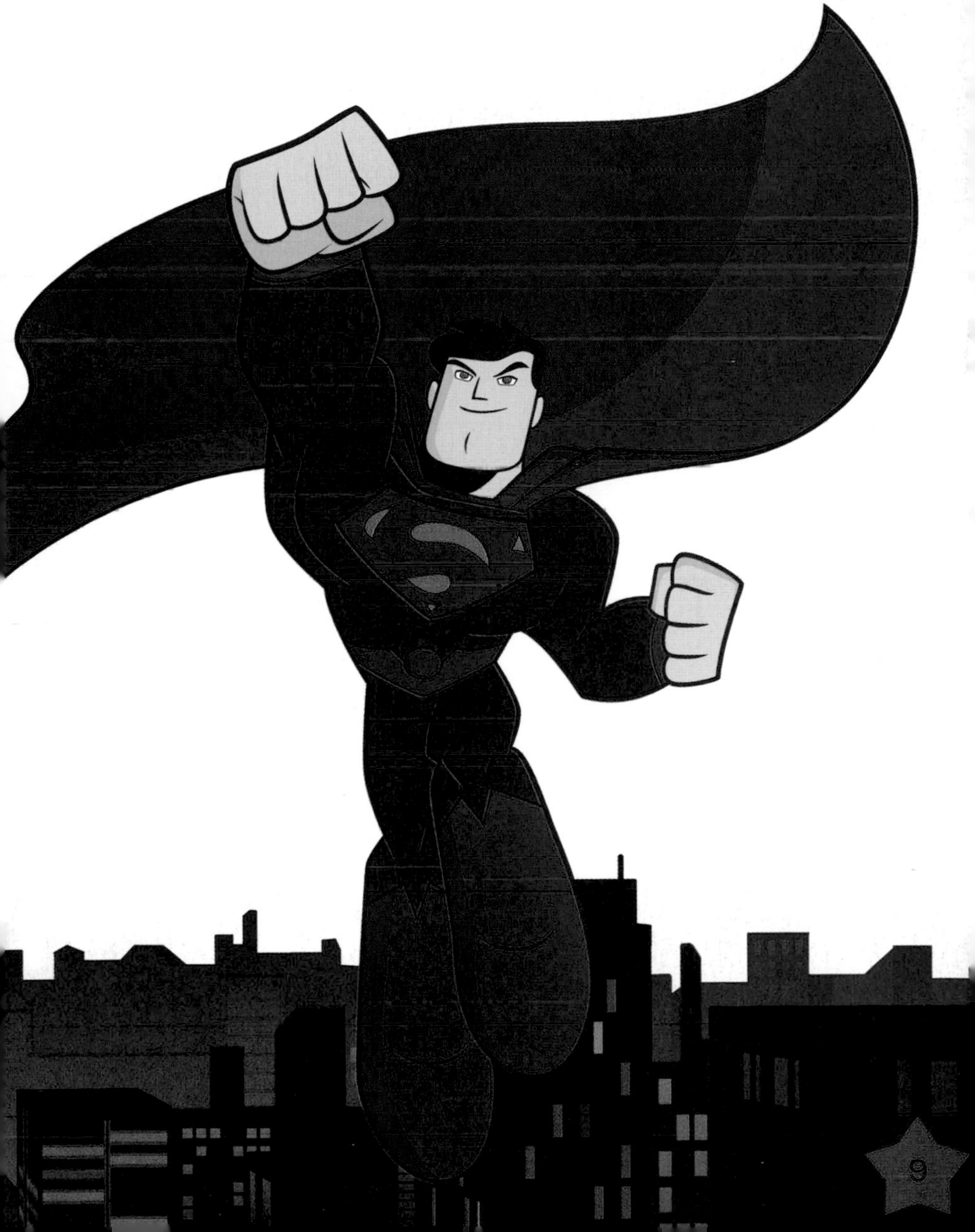

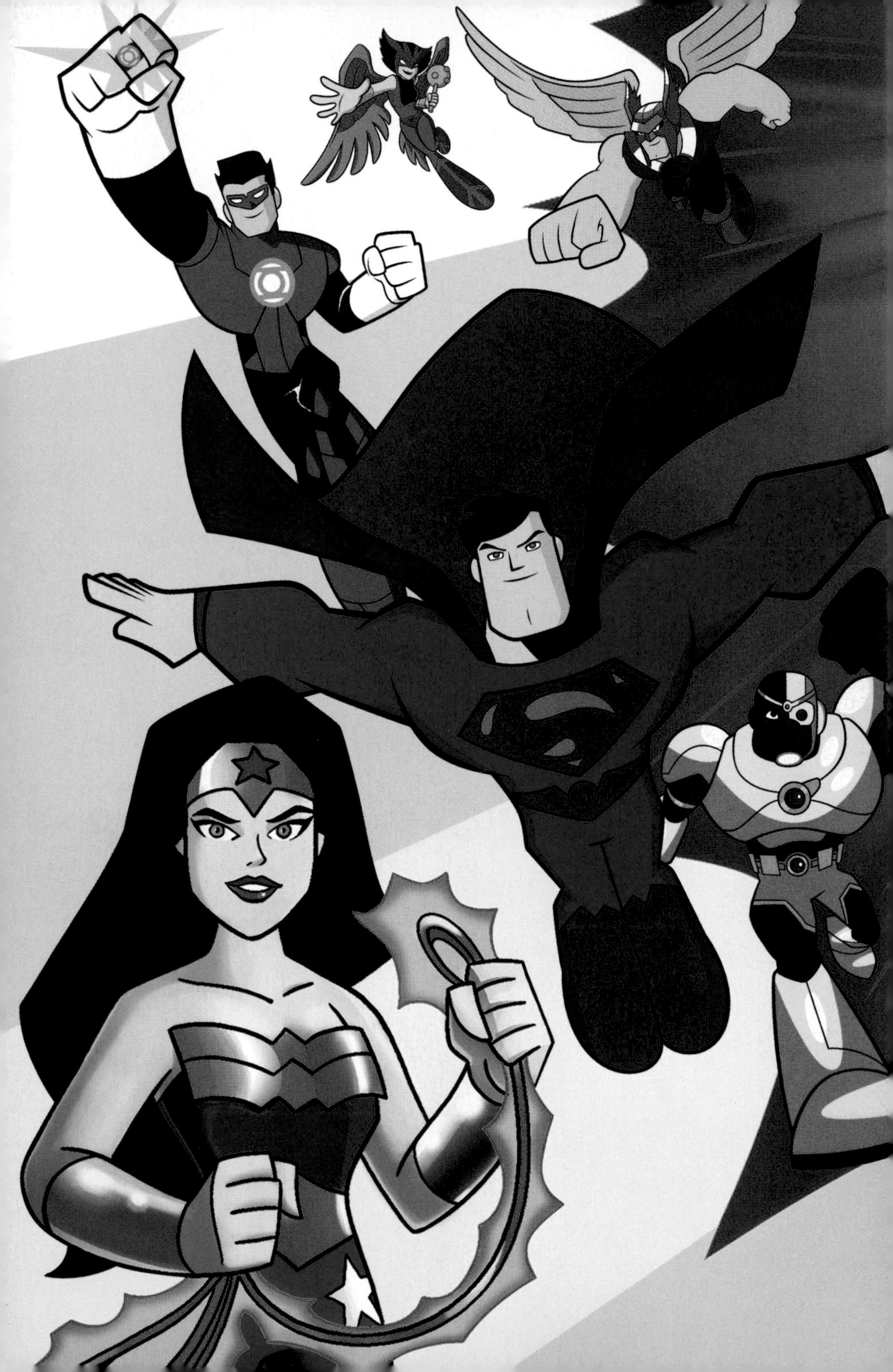

MEET THE DC SUPER FRIENDS!

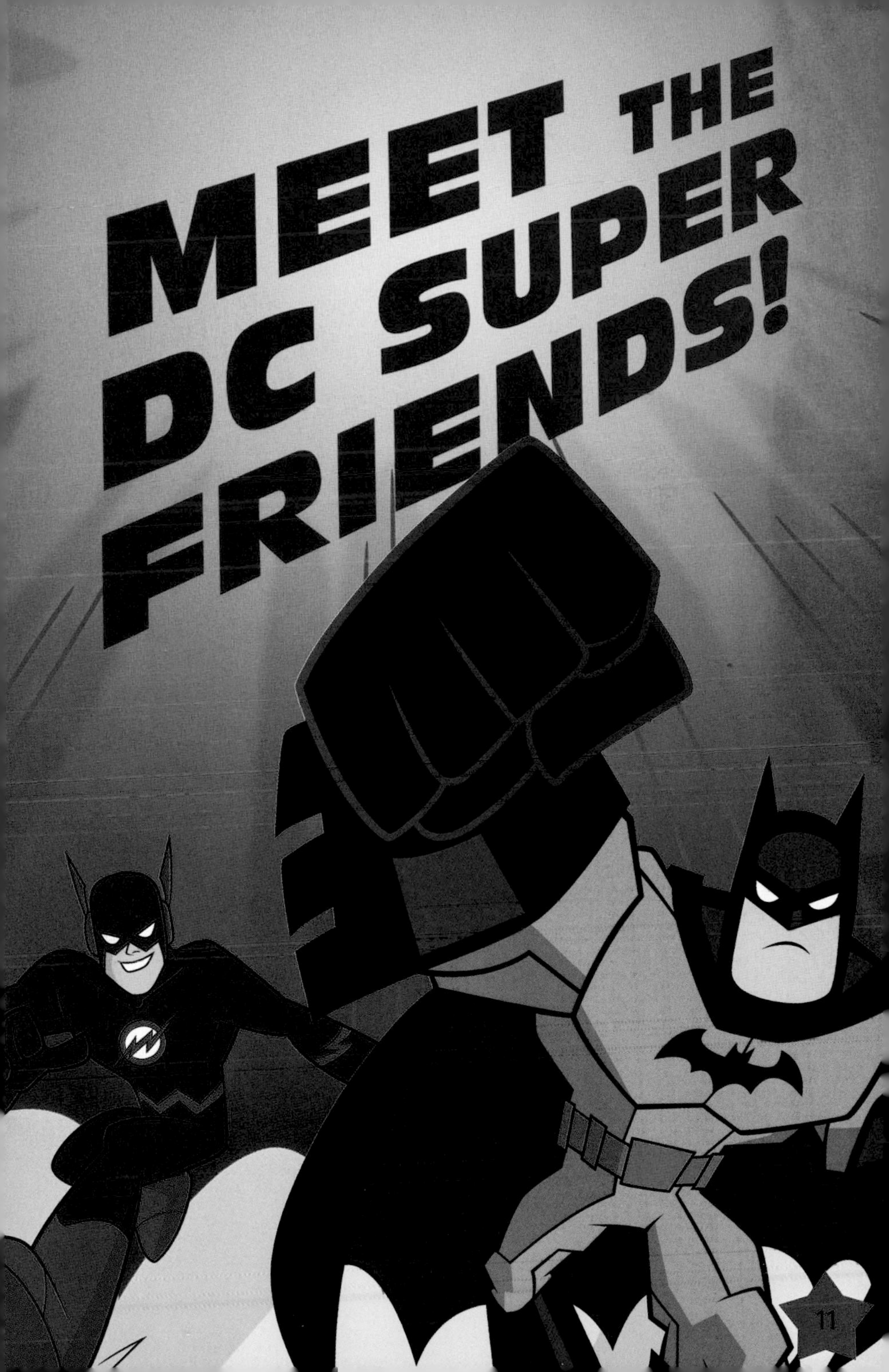

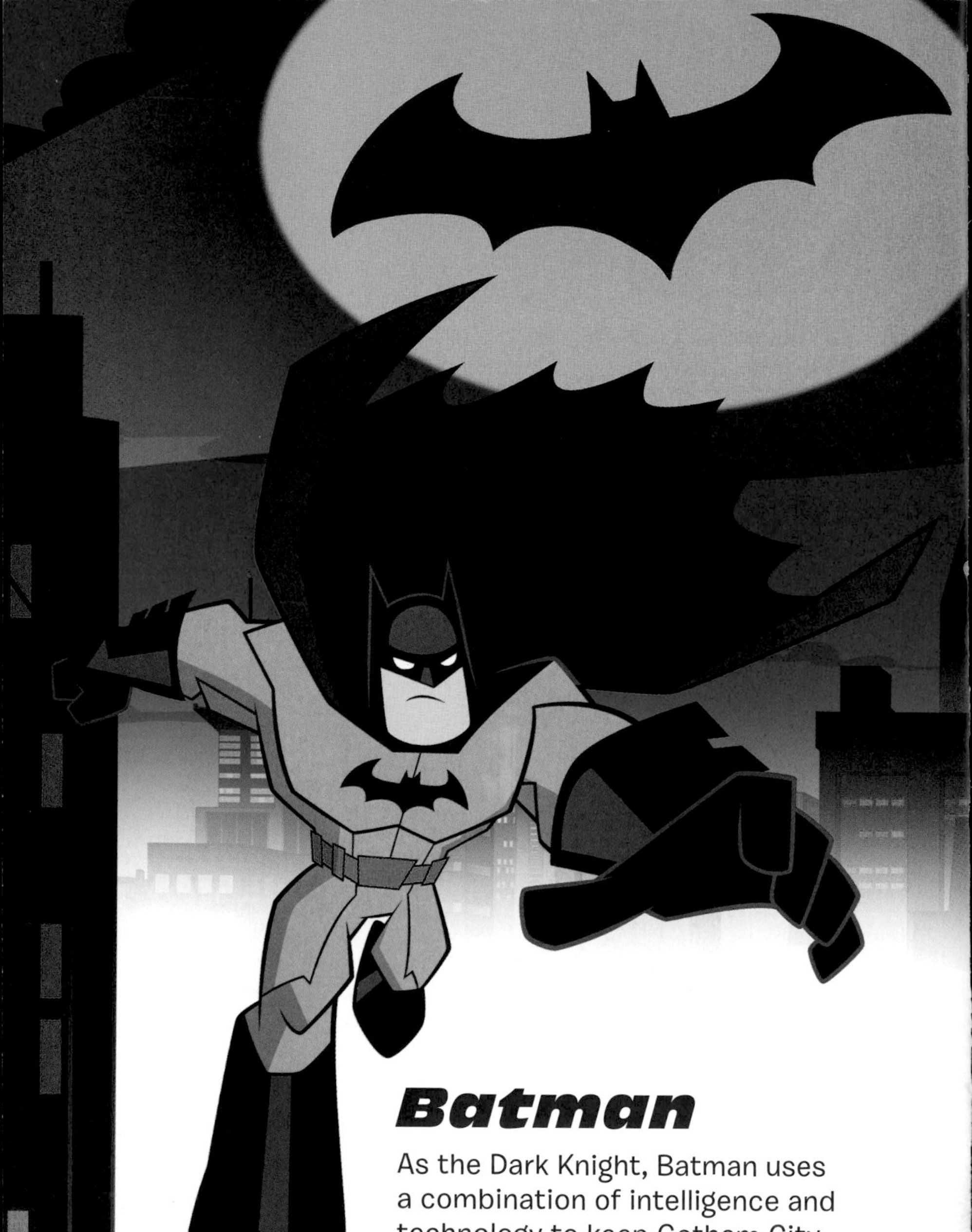

Batman

As the Dark Knight, Batman uses a combination of intelligence and technology to keep Gotham City safe from criminals and super-villains.

Robin

The Boy Wonder is an amazing acrobat who is Batman's partner in fighting crime.

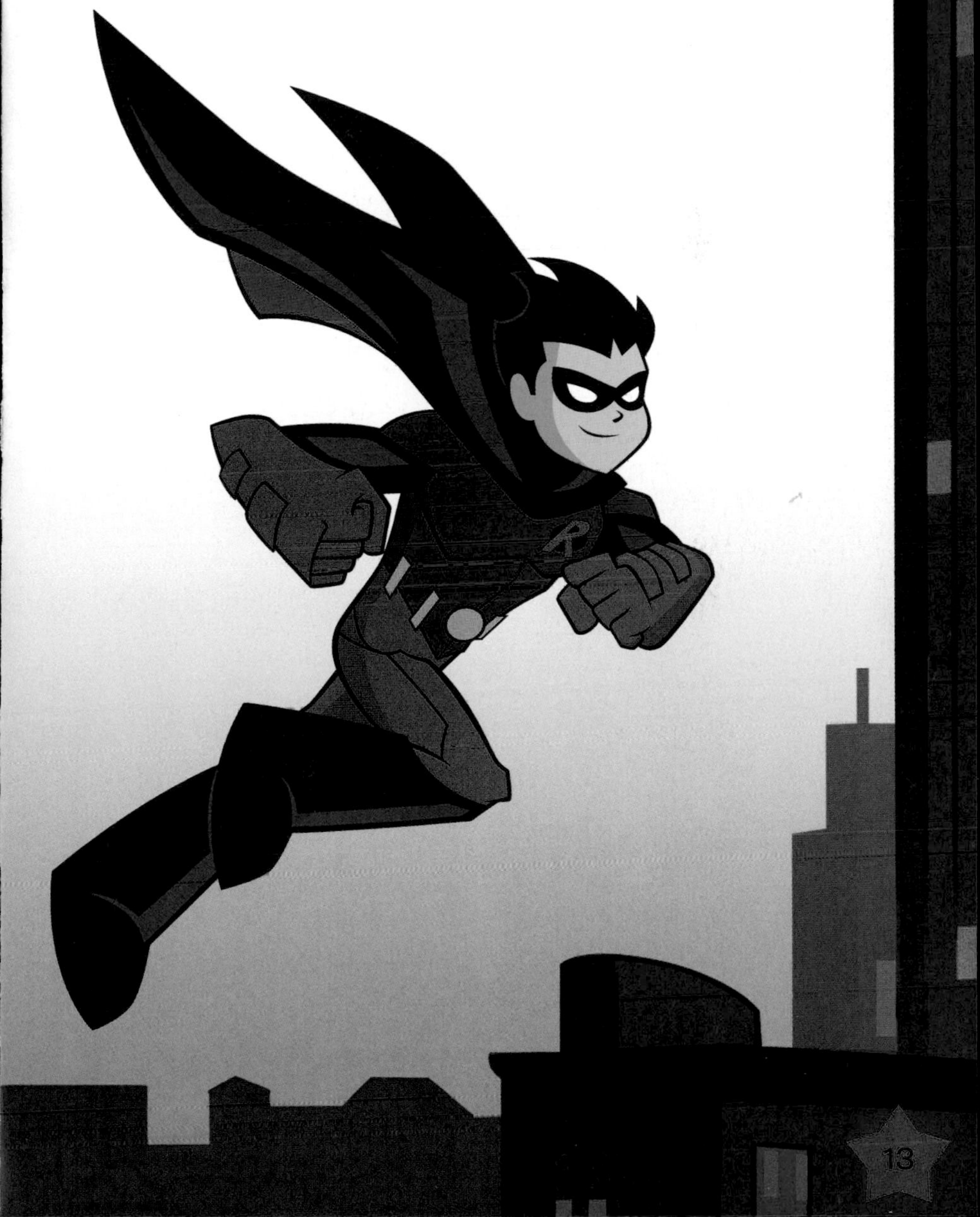

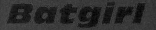

Batgirl

This daring defender uses her advanced computer and karate skills to repel the forces of evil.

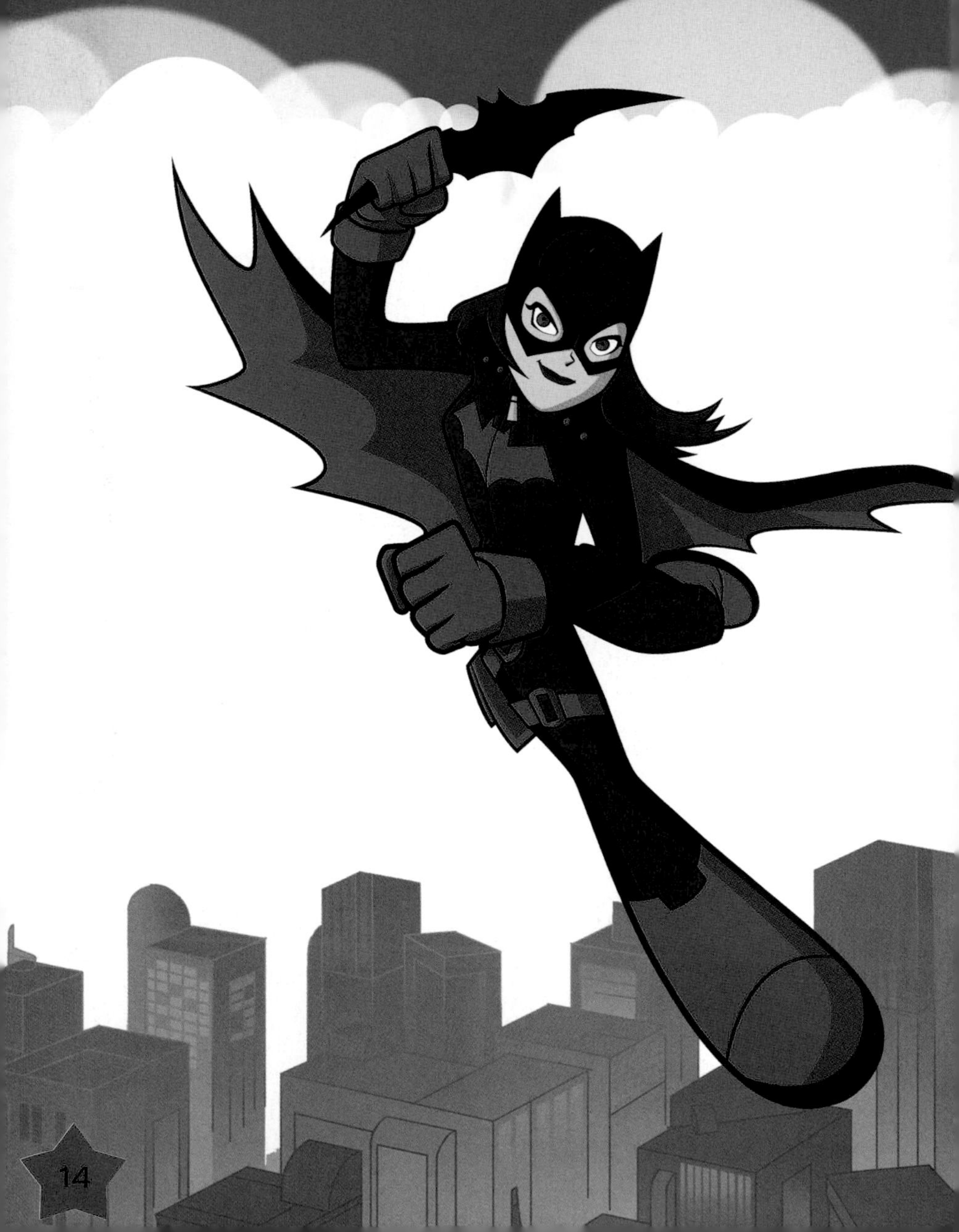

Wonder Woman

This Amazon princess uses her amazing strength and Golden Lasso in the pursuit of truth and justice for all.

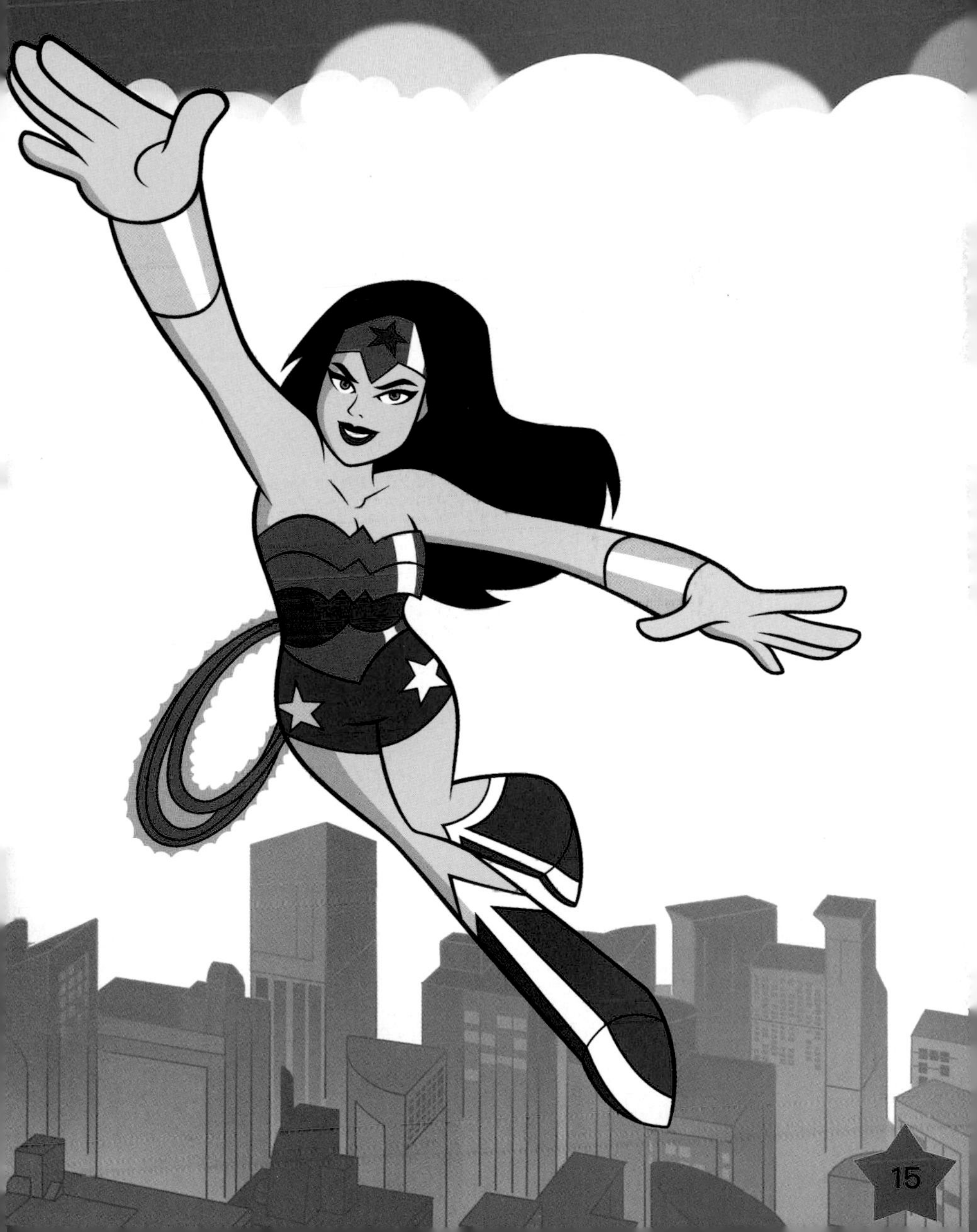

Superman

With his amazing superpowers, the Man of Steel is an indestructible alien who protects the planet Earth from every kind of threat.

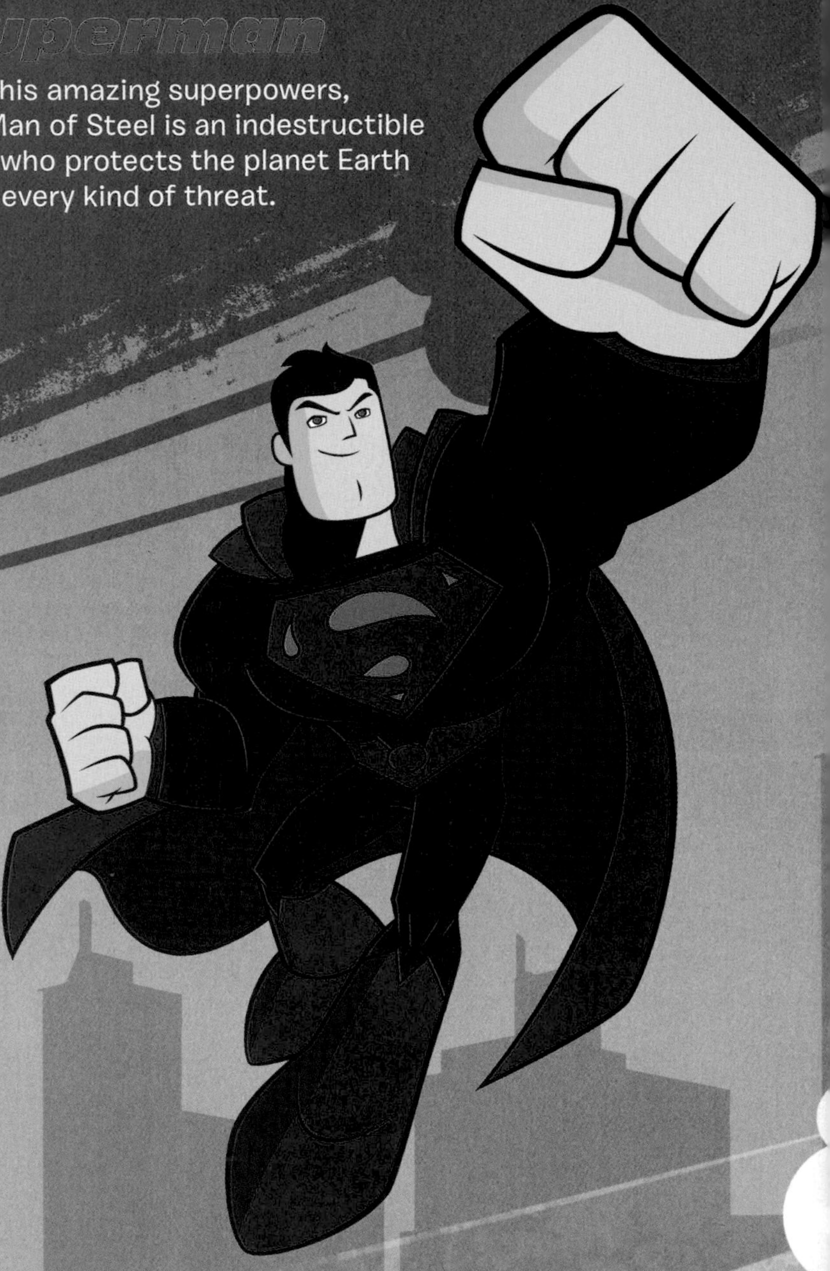

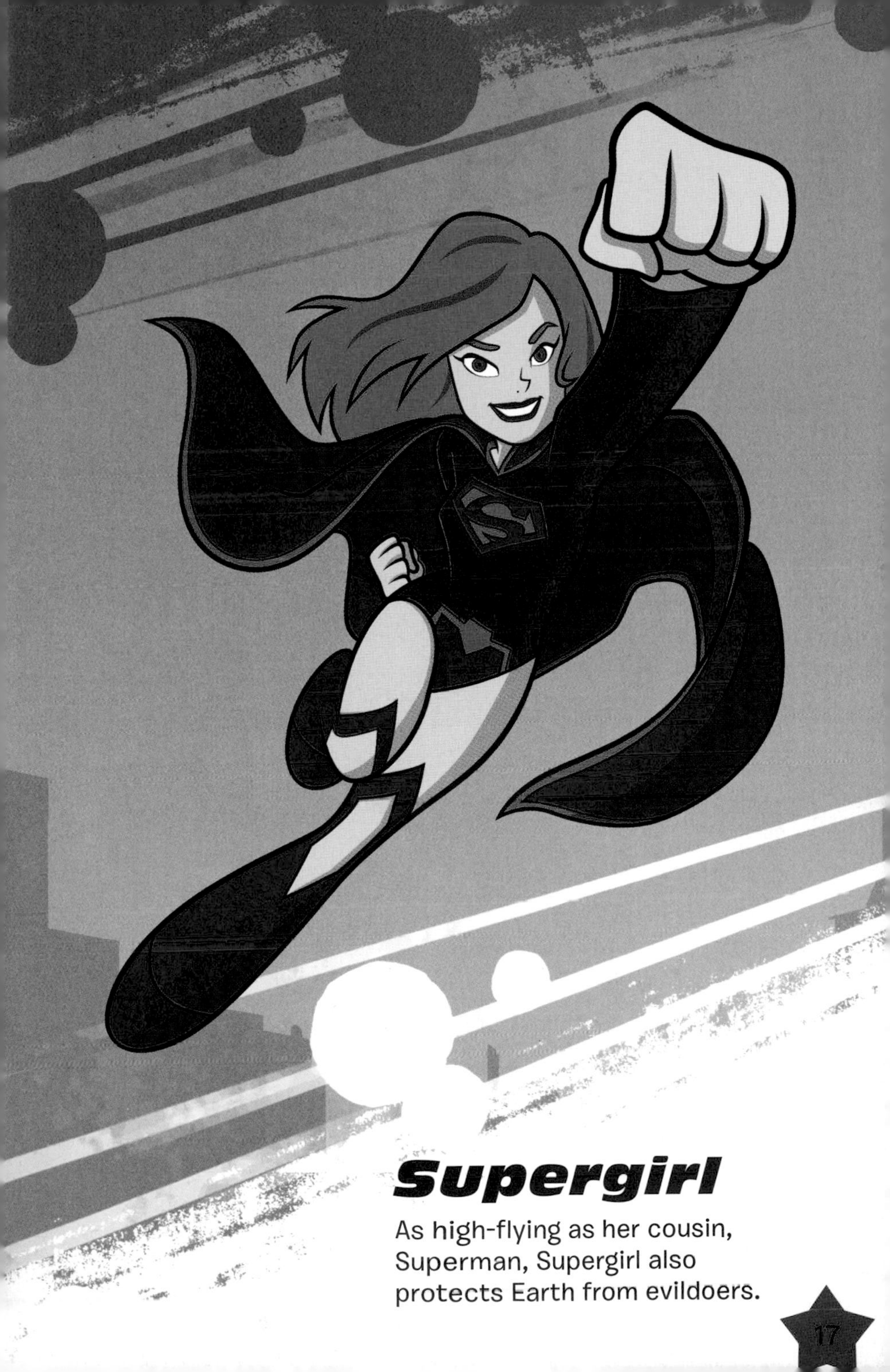

Supergirl

As high-flying as her cousin, Superman, Supergirl also protects Earth from evildoers.

Green Arrow

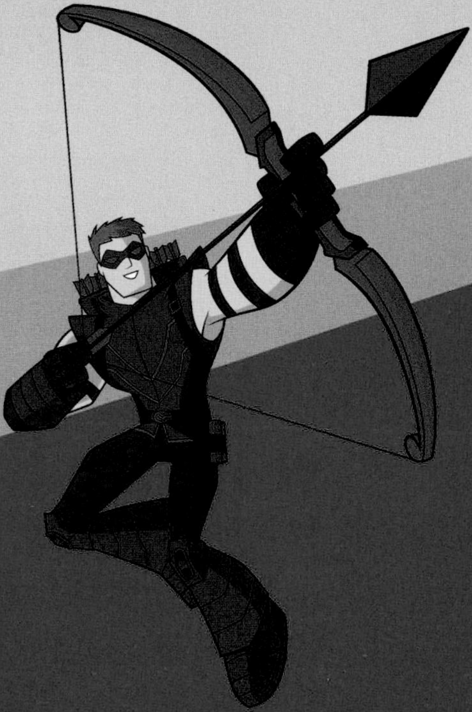

The Emerald Archer uses his extraordinary archery expertise and quick wit to bring in the bad guys.

Green Lantern

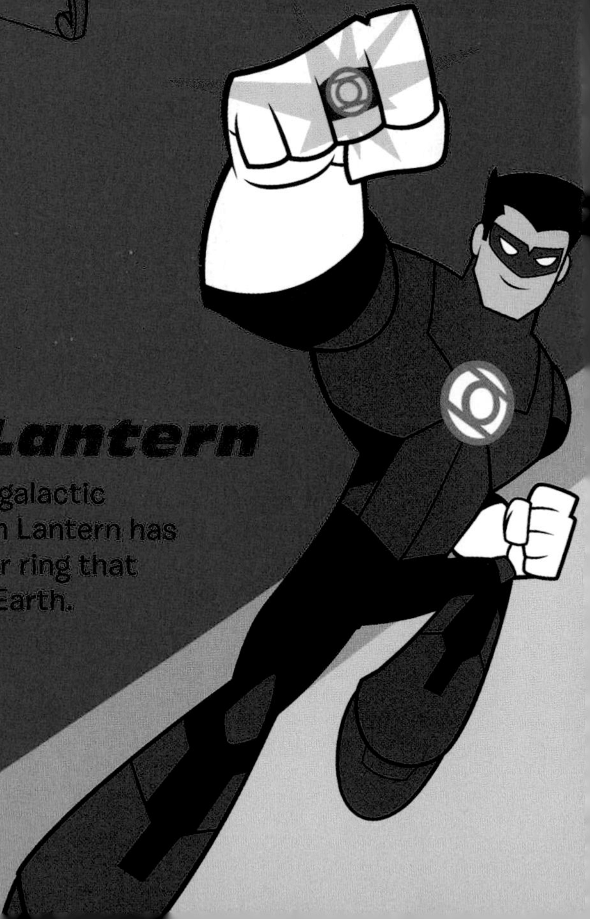

As part of an intergalactic police force, Green Lantern has been given a power ring that helps him defend Earth.

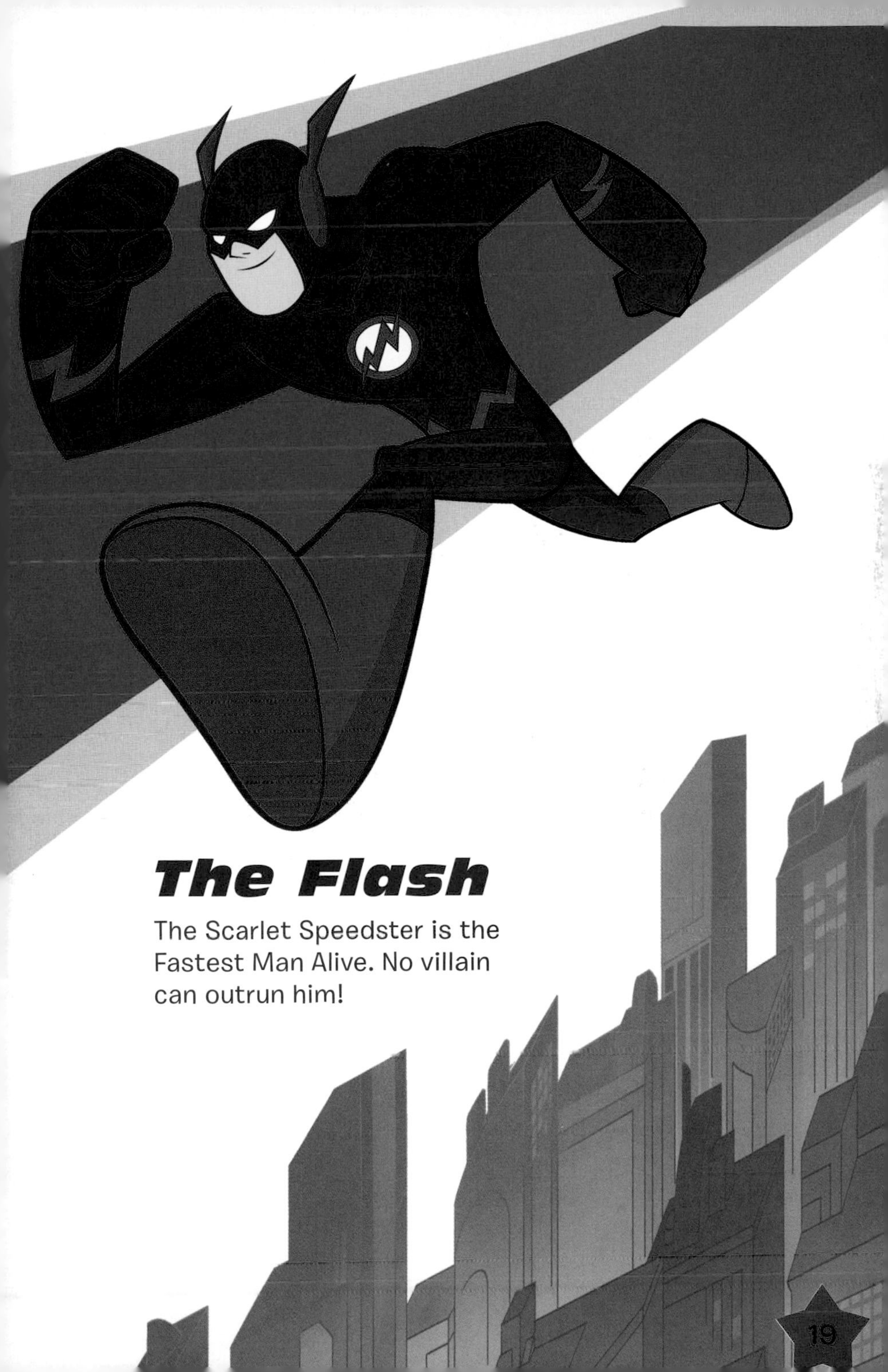

The Flash

The Scarlet Speedster is the Fastest Man Alive. No villain can outrun him!

Cyborg

Part man, part high-tech machine, Cyborg is an advanced living weapon.

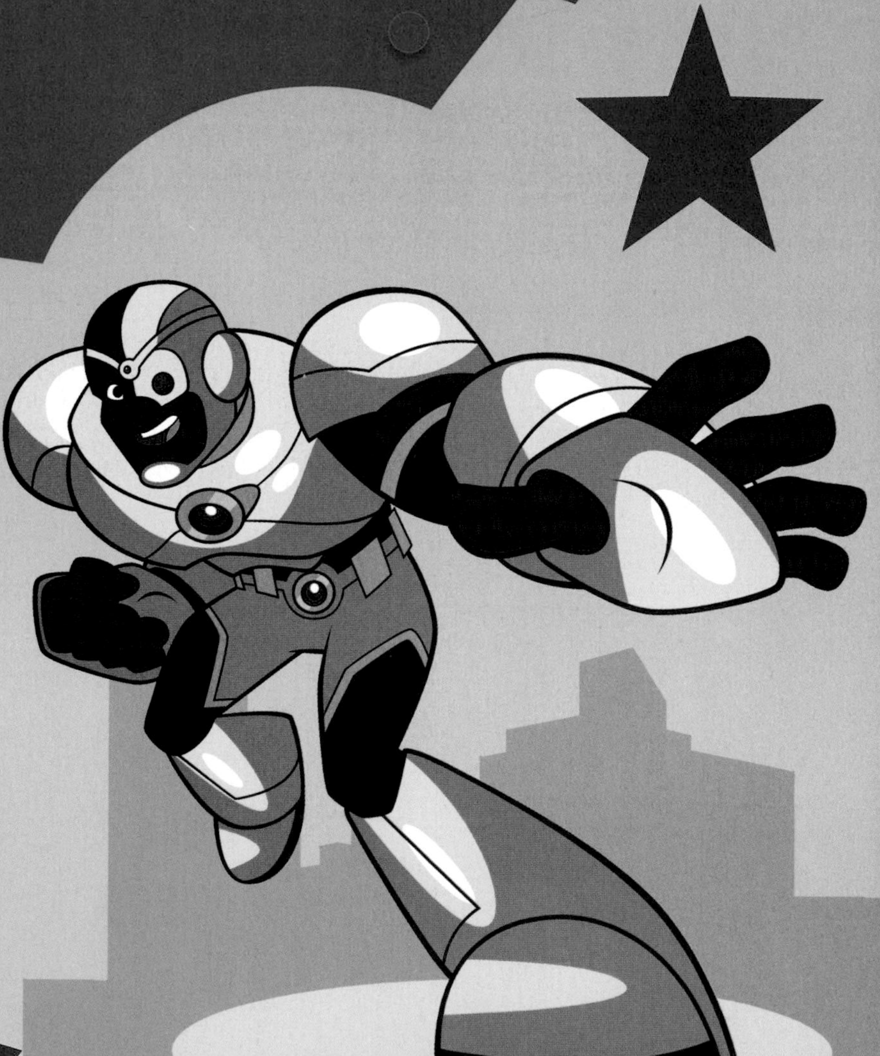

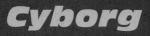

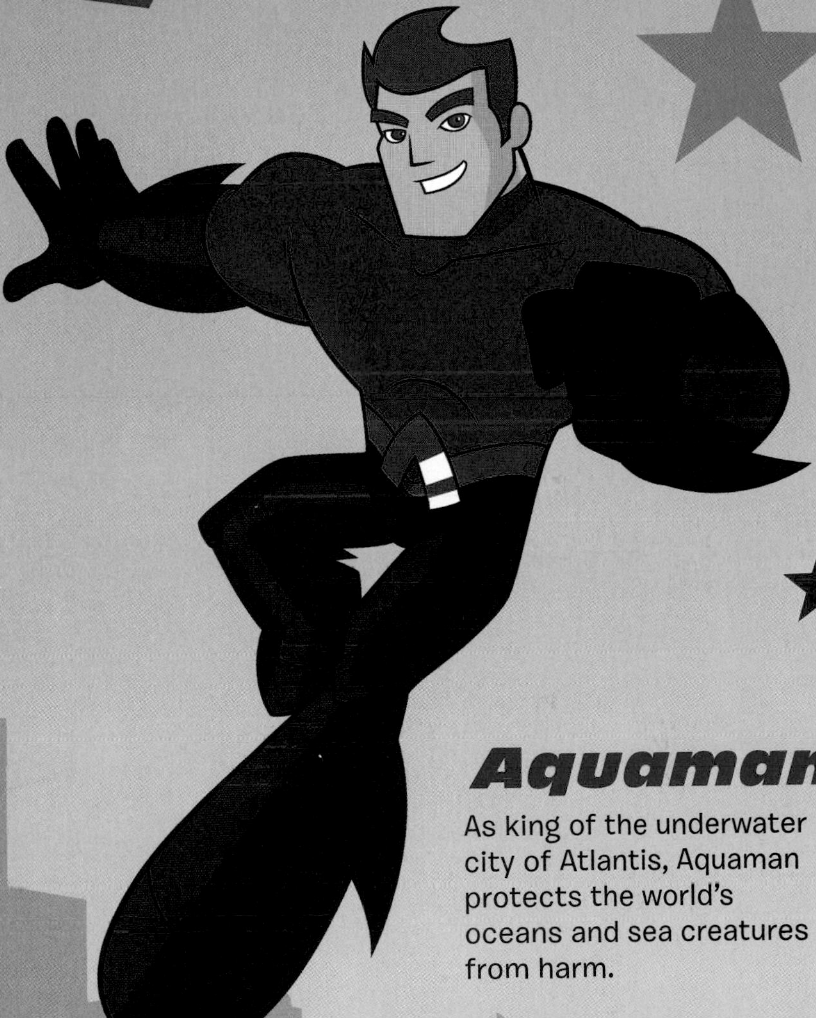

Aquaman

As king of the underwater city of Atlantis, Aquaman protects the world's oceans and sea creatures from harm.

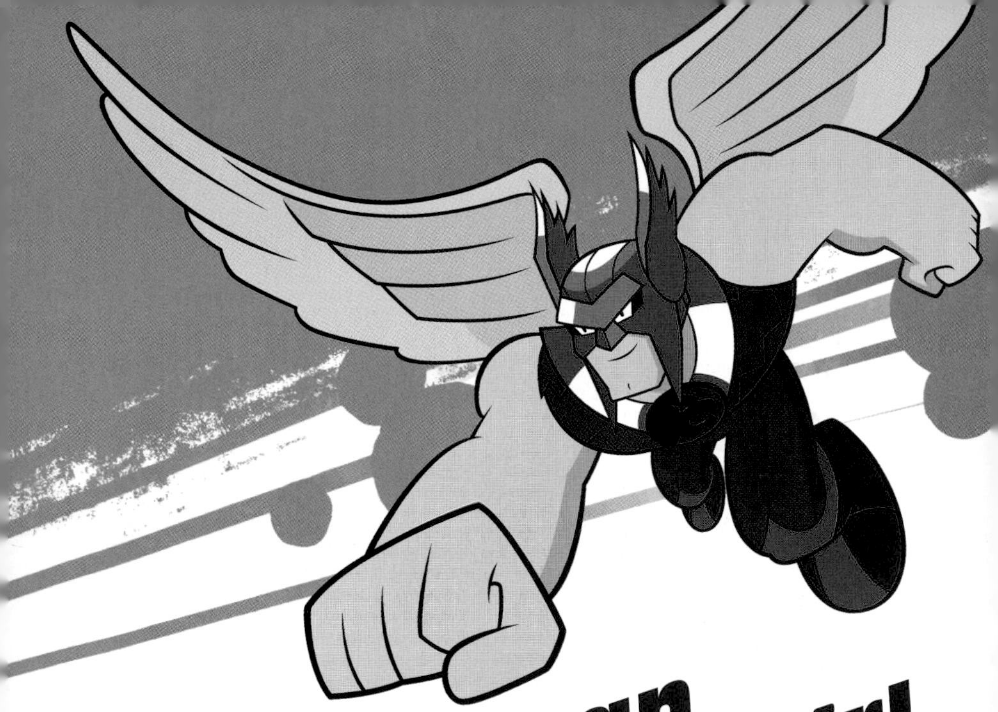

Hawkman and Hawkgirl

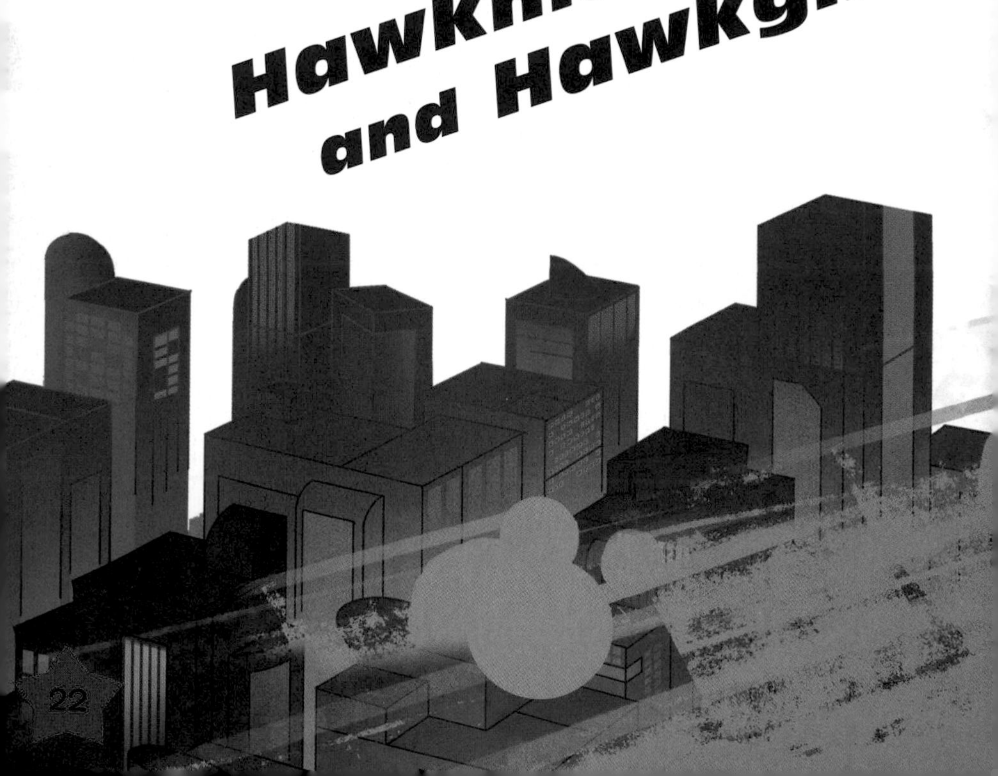

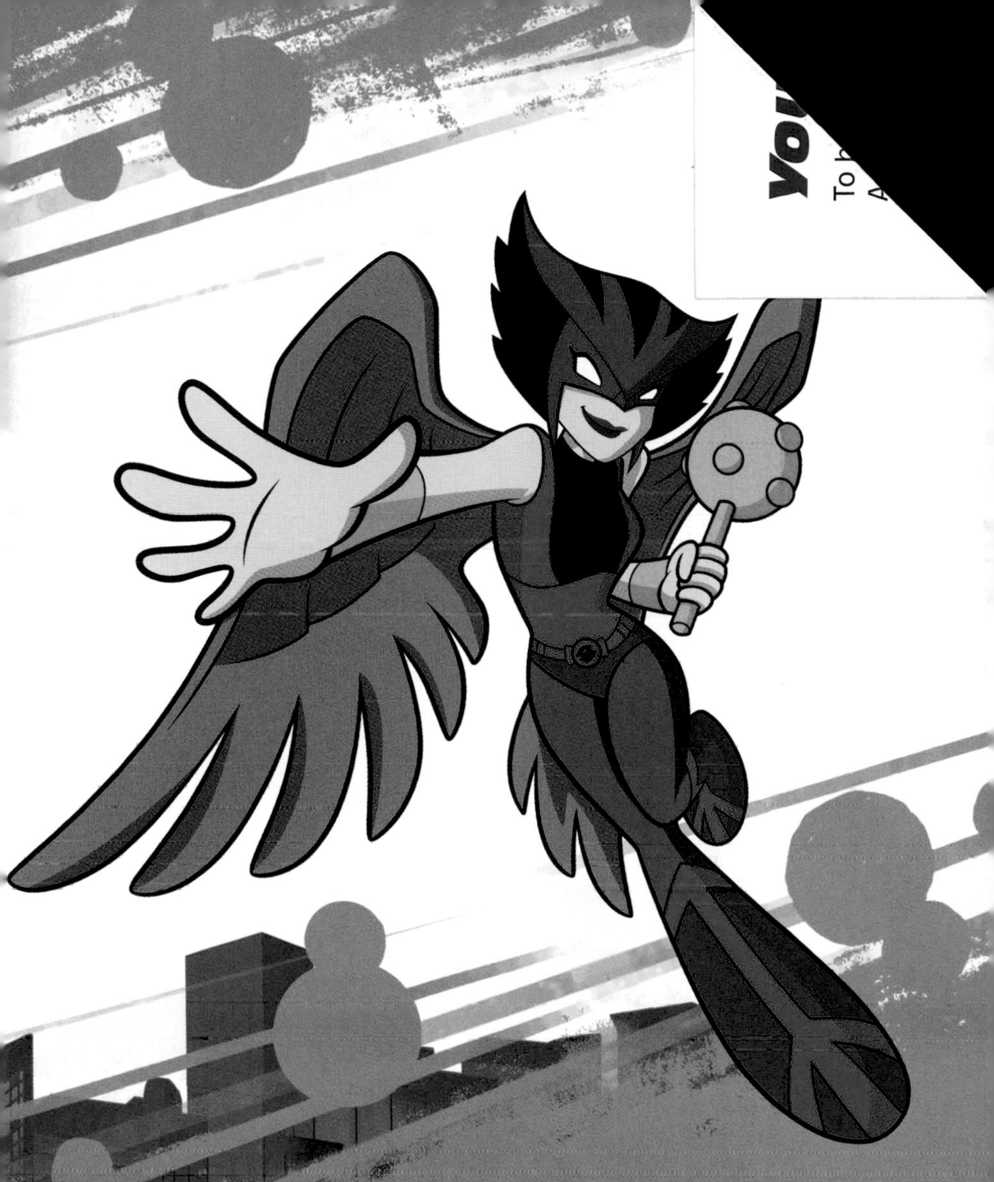

These winged warriors patrol the skies on the lookout for trouble. Few villains can withstand the blows from their mighty maces.

r Super Hero Name

e like the Super Friends, you'll need a heroic name!
good name meets the following criteria:

Be Original

Pick a name no one else has.
If you look online, you don't
want to find other heroes
with the same name!

Be Powerful

Pick a strong, bold name
that will make people feel safe
yet strike fear in the frozen
hearts of super-villains
everywhere!

Be Unique

Pick a name that showcases
your personality and
individuality.

These names all contain clues that point to the kind of hero each Super Friend is. Your name can do this, too! Check out the suggestions on the next page for ideas.

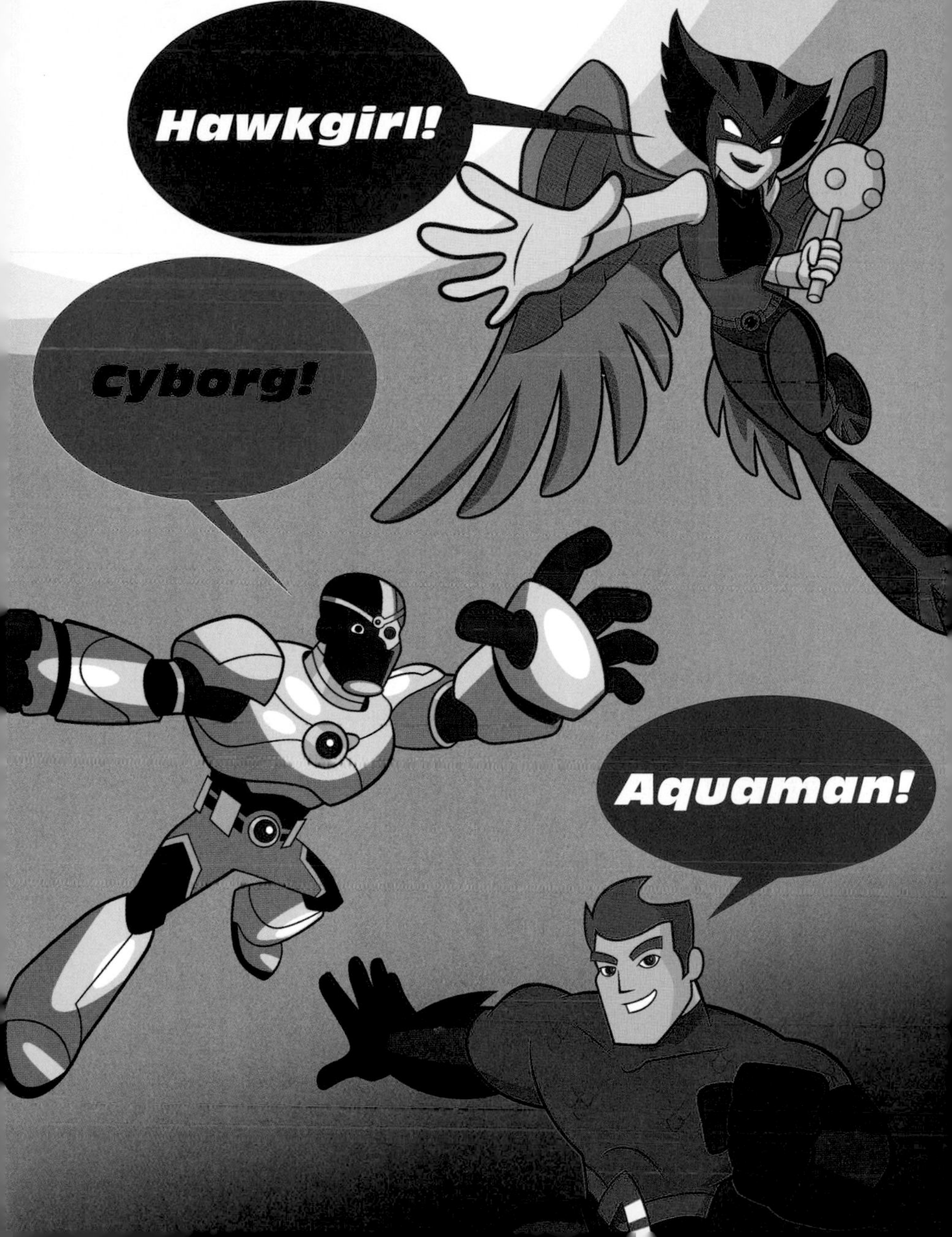
Hawkgirl!
Cyborg!
Aquaman!

Creating a Super Hero Name

Hero names are often a combination of elements. Try choosing several different words from the following categories. Then you can narrow down your favorites to create a super hero name!

All About You

Examples: favorite hobbies, sports, songs, movies, books, animals, or foods

Positive Descriptors

Examples: amazing, astounding, astonishing, remarkable, wonderful, incredible, marvelous, surprising, stupendous, noble, valiant, brave, courageous

Action or Sound Words

Examples: crash, power, stun, siren, bam

Random Words You Like

Examples: pony, sunshine, money, talent, mermaid, cowboy, vampire, werewolf

Add a Color

Examples: red, orange, yellow, green, blue, pink, purple, black, brown, white, gold, silver, platinum, chrome, rainbow

Formal Title

Examples: Mr., Mrs., Ms., Miss, Dr., Admiral, Professor, Dame, Lady, Lord, Madam, Sir, Commander, Colonel, Prince, Princess, Woman, Man, Guy, Girl, Boy, Kid

Feel free to try out names until you find one that's just right for your super hero identity. Good-Guy Man? Professor Periwinkle? Ms. Pizza Girl? Fluffy-Kitten Kid? Whatever works for you!

And make sure to keep track of your rejected names so you can pass one on to your sidekick!

Special Powers

Every super hero needs a set of superpowers or skills. Just because you weren't born with meta-human strength or the ability to scale skyscrapers doesn't mean you can't be a hero. Start by focusing on what you're really good at and what you want to achieve to figure out how to hone your super skills.

Physical Strength: Exercise, exercise, exercise!

Speed: Run on a treadmill or around the block to increase your speed and stamina. You'll never outrun The Flash by sitting in front of a TV or computer screen all day!

Stealth: Practice being light on your feet so no one hears you coming.

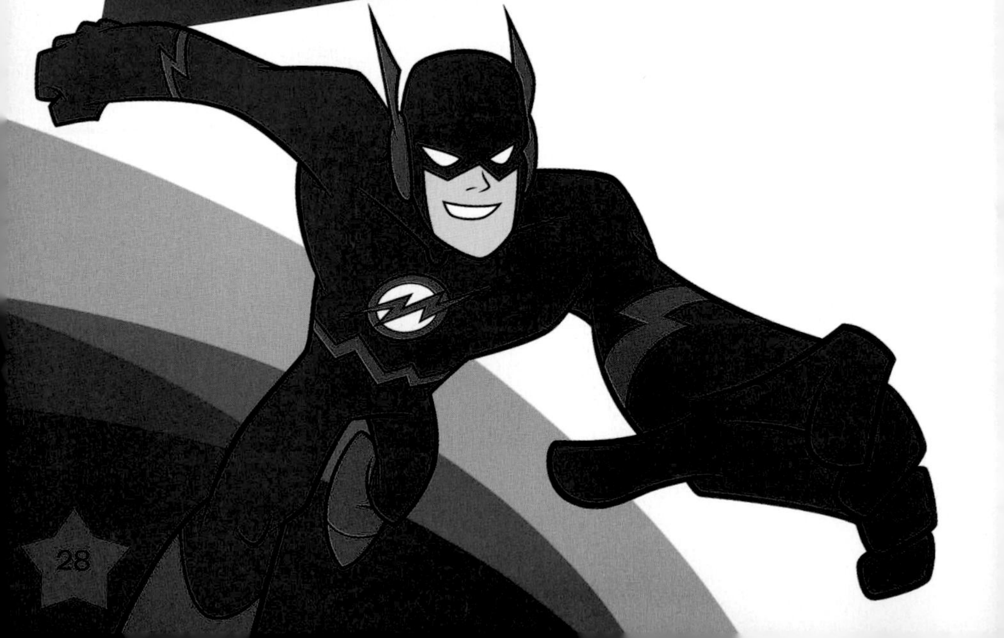

Regeneration and Immunity: Eat a healthy diet full of fruits and vegetables, get at least eight hours of sleep per night, drink lots of water, and be sure to visit the doctor and the dentist regularly.

Agility and Skills: Practice gymnastics or yoga. Learn new skills, such as archery, martial arts, or computer science.

Brains: Study hard in school and read books, newspapers, and other articles online. Developing your mind and unlocking your brainpower are essential weapons in your arsenal.

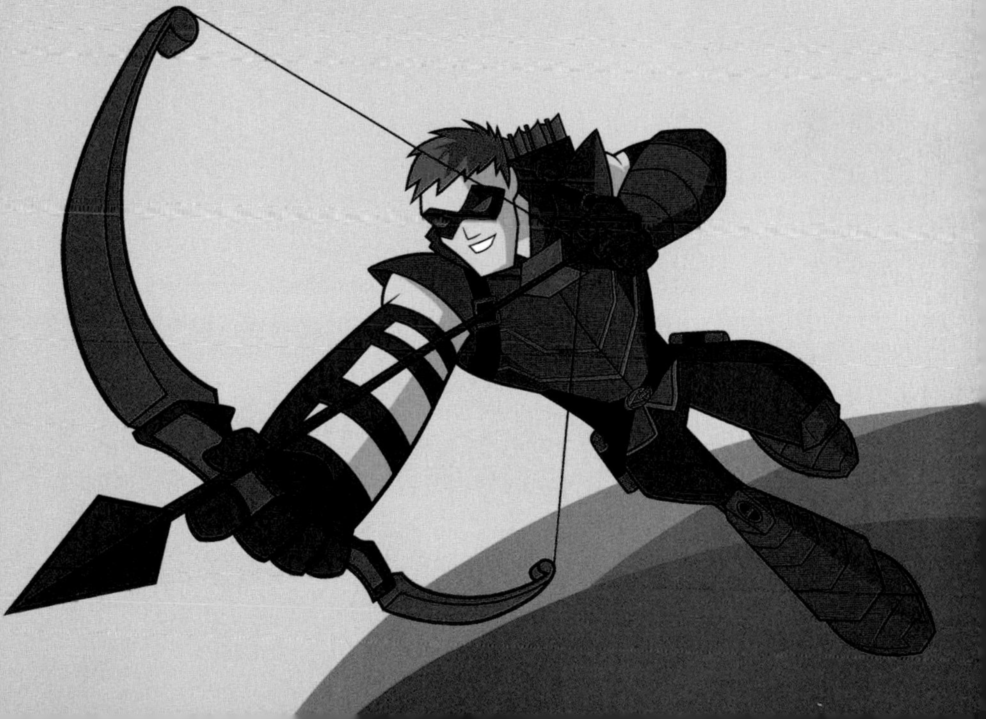

Costume Design

Coming up with a costume design is one of the most fun parts of being a super hero! To start, think about what kind of costume would help you achieve your goals.

Costume Style

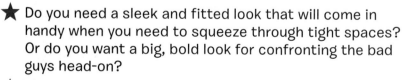

★ Do you want a material that's light and airy, that won't weigh you down when you're racing to the rescue? Or do you want heavy armor to protect you from lasers, missiles, and powerful punches?

★ Do you need a sleek and fitted look that will come in handy when you need to squeeze through tight spaces? Or do you want a big, bold look for confronting the bad guys head-on?

★ Be sure that it's easy to assemble and perfect for a quick change on the go!

Color Scheme

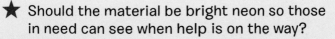

★ Should the material be bright neon so those in need can see when help is on the way?

★ Should it be metallic to show that you're ready to shine?

★ Should the fabric be dark camouflage to help you sneak around in the shadows at night?

31

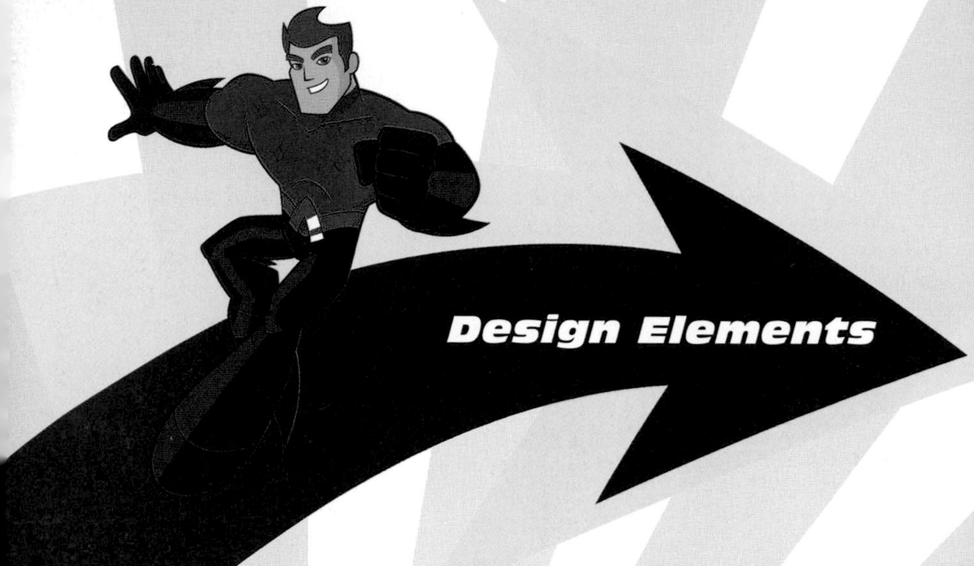

Design Elements

- Do you want to add stars, stripes, polka dots, hearts, lightning bolts, or flames? The design elements should reflect your heroic persona.
- Should you add letters or a logo to your costume so you are easily identifiable?

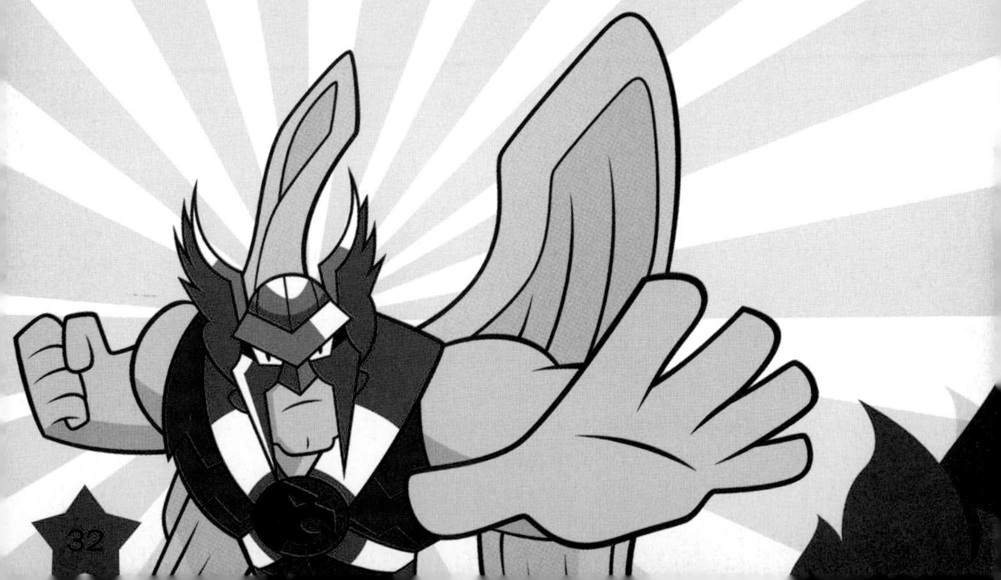

Costume Add-Ons

⚡ Will you wear a cape, like Superman and Supergirl?

⚡ Should you add a mysterious mask, like Batman and Batgirl?

⚡ How about a special ring, like the Green Lantern, or metallic bracelets and a tiara, like Wonder Woman?

All these things are important to keep in mind when you're brainstorming costume ideas. Whatever you decide, make sure you have something that's easy to wash and maintain. There's no time for a trip to the dry cleaner when you have a whole world to save!

Logos and Symbols

A good logo or symbol is important. You'll need to create something specific and memorable that's easy to recognize and that warns bad guys you're ready to save the day. Start with a basic shape—circle, oval, heart, diamond, or shield—and then add elements that showcase your individuality.

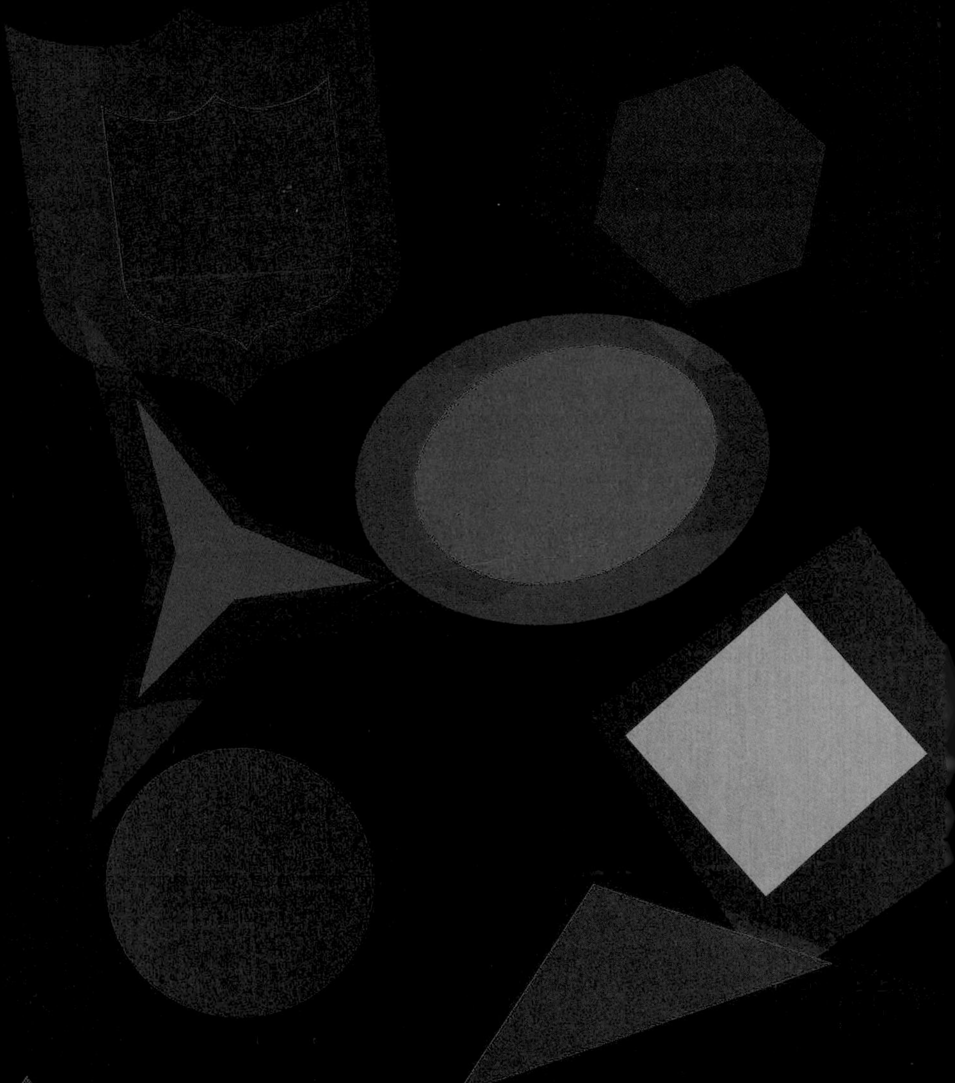

Batman: The bat-symbol is one of the best-known logos in the world. It strikes fear in the hearts of villains everywhere!

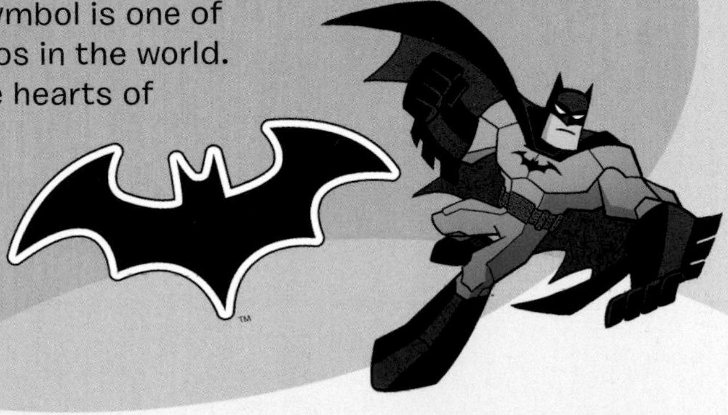

Superman: The emblem on Superman's chest includes a big, bold **S**. It is the ultimate symbol of hope and goodness.

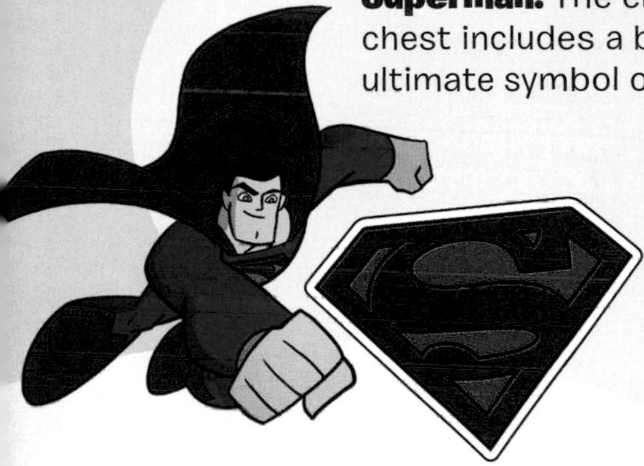

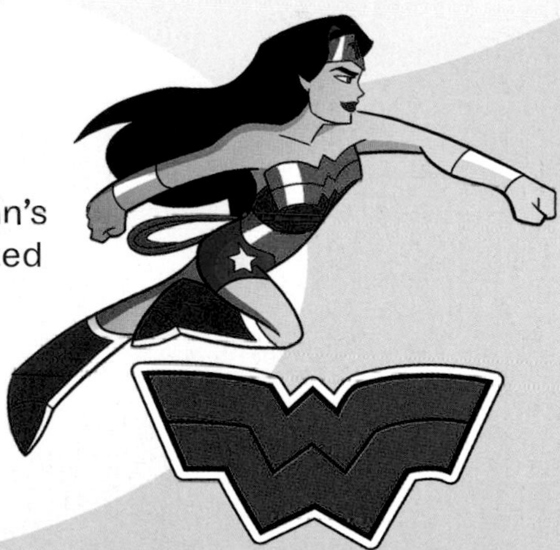

Wonder Woman: Wonder Woman's symbol consists of two connected **W**s and wings, which symbolize her name and her ability to fly.

How will your logo look? Try lots of designs!

Mottoes, Slogans, and Catchphrases

Now that you have your super hero symbol, you're ready to come up with a good catchphrase, such as "Don't worry! Help is on the way!" Make sure it's not too complicated, because you'll have to remember it when you're saving the day.

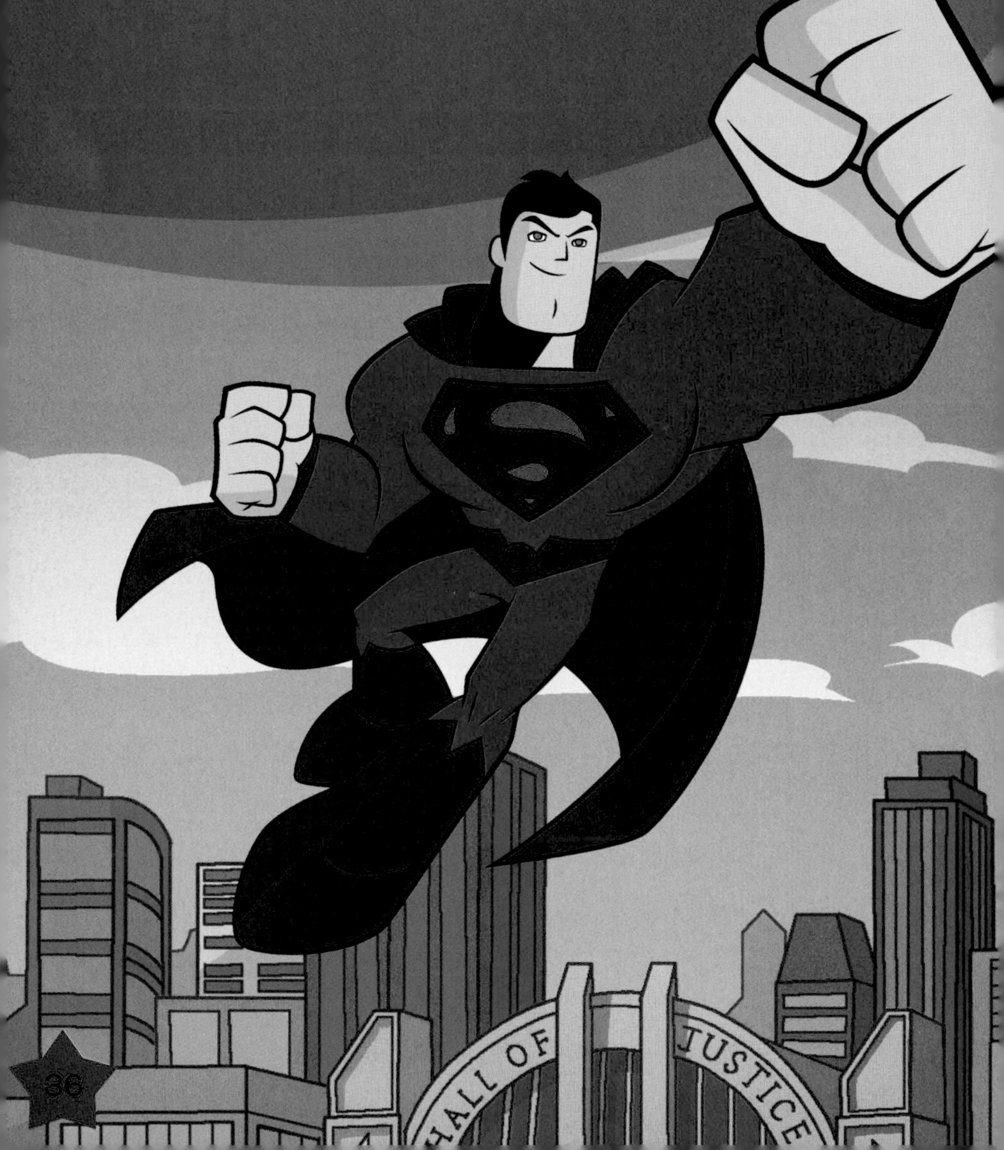
HALL OF JUSTICE

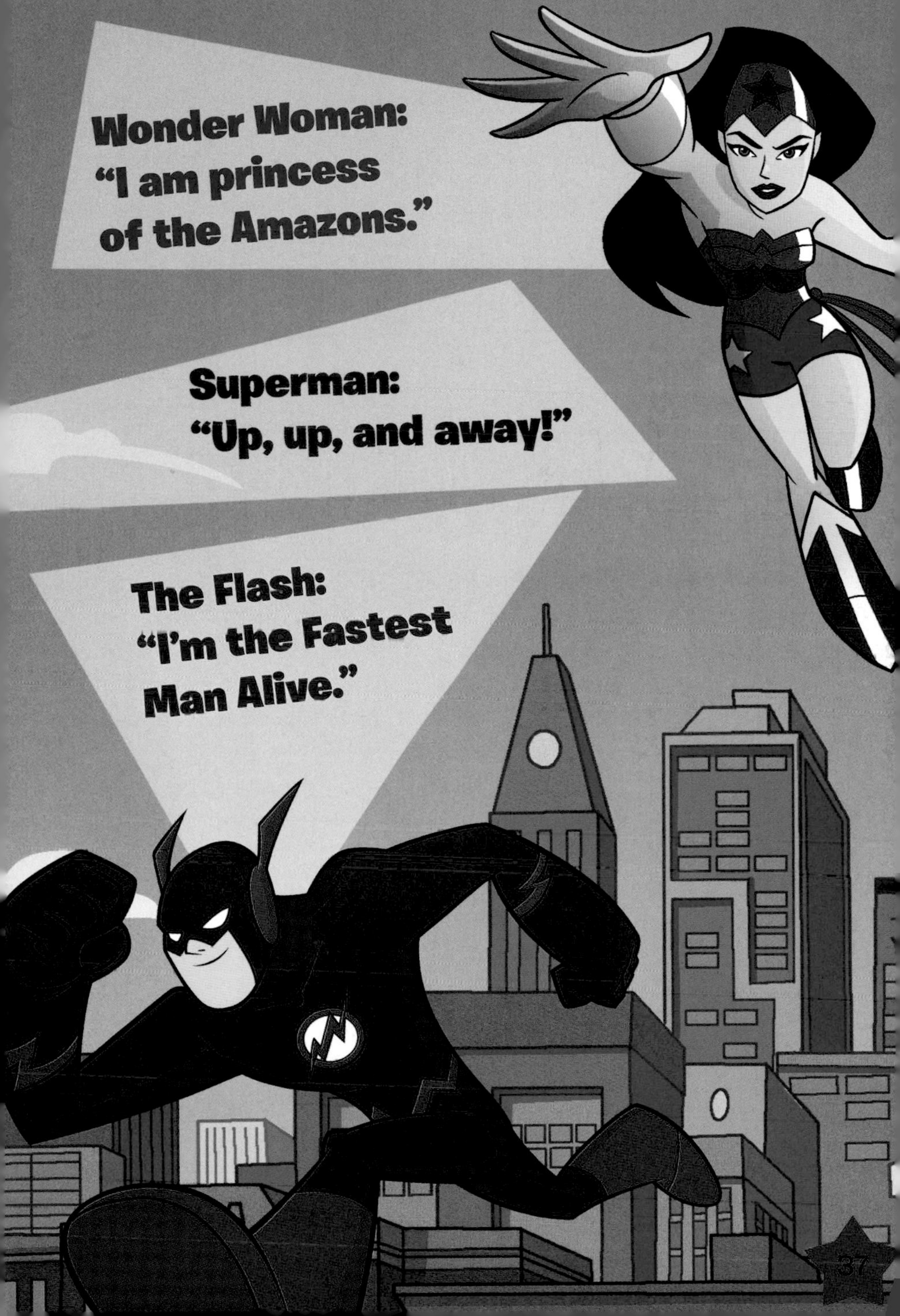
Wonder Woman: "I am princess of the Amazons."
Superman: "Up, up, and away!"
The Flash: "I'm the Fastest Man Alive."

Choosing a Sidekick

When you're a hero, it's essential to know who can and cannot be trusted with your heroic identity and crime-solving secrets. Remember—once you tell people the truth, you can never *un*tell them!

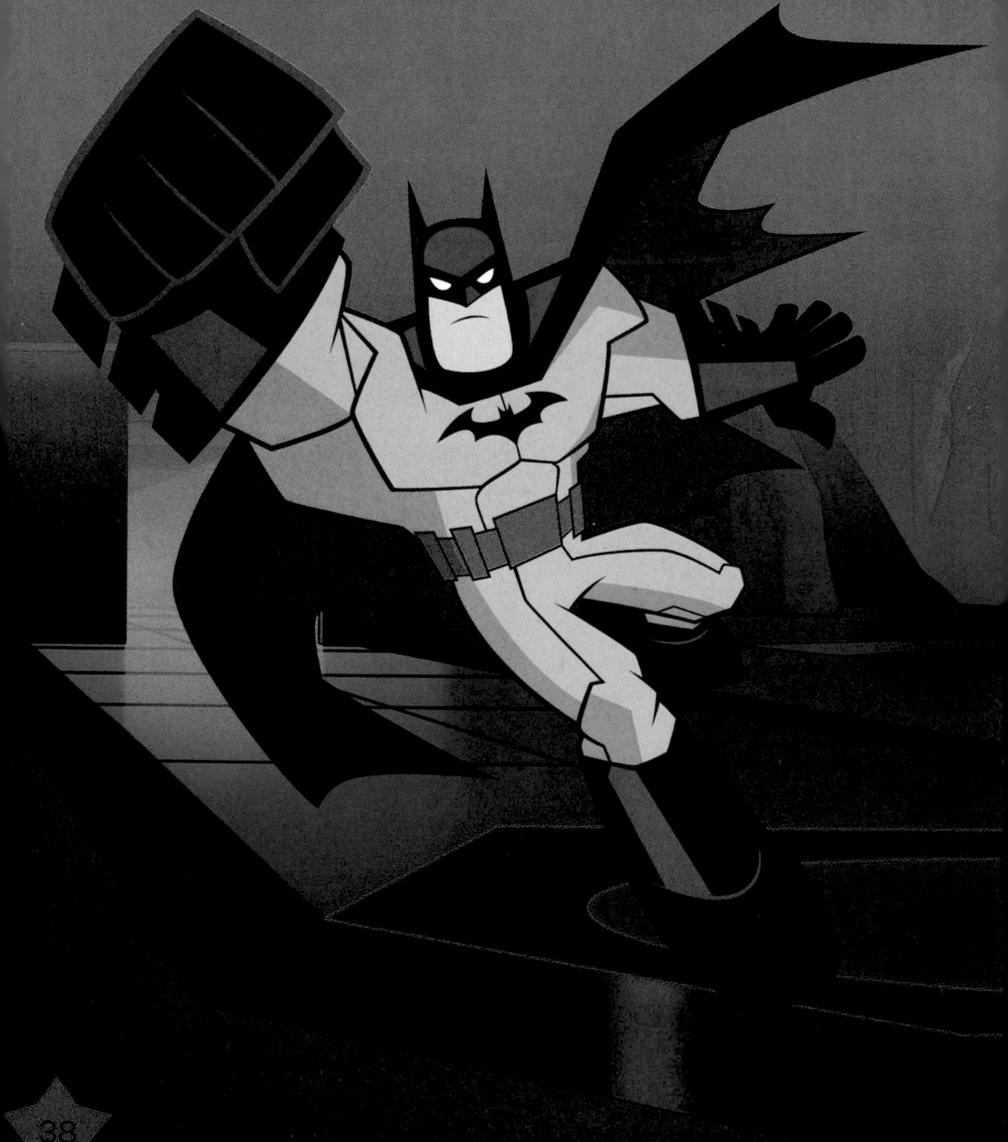

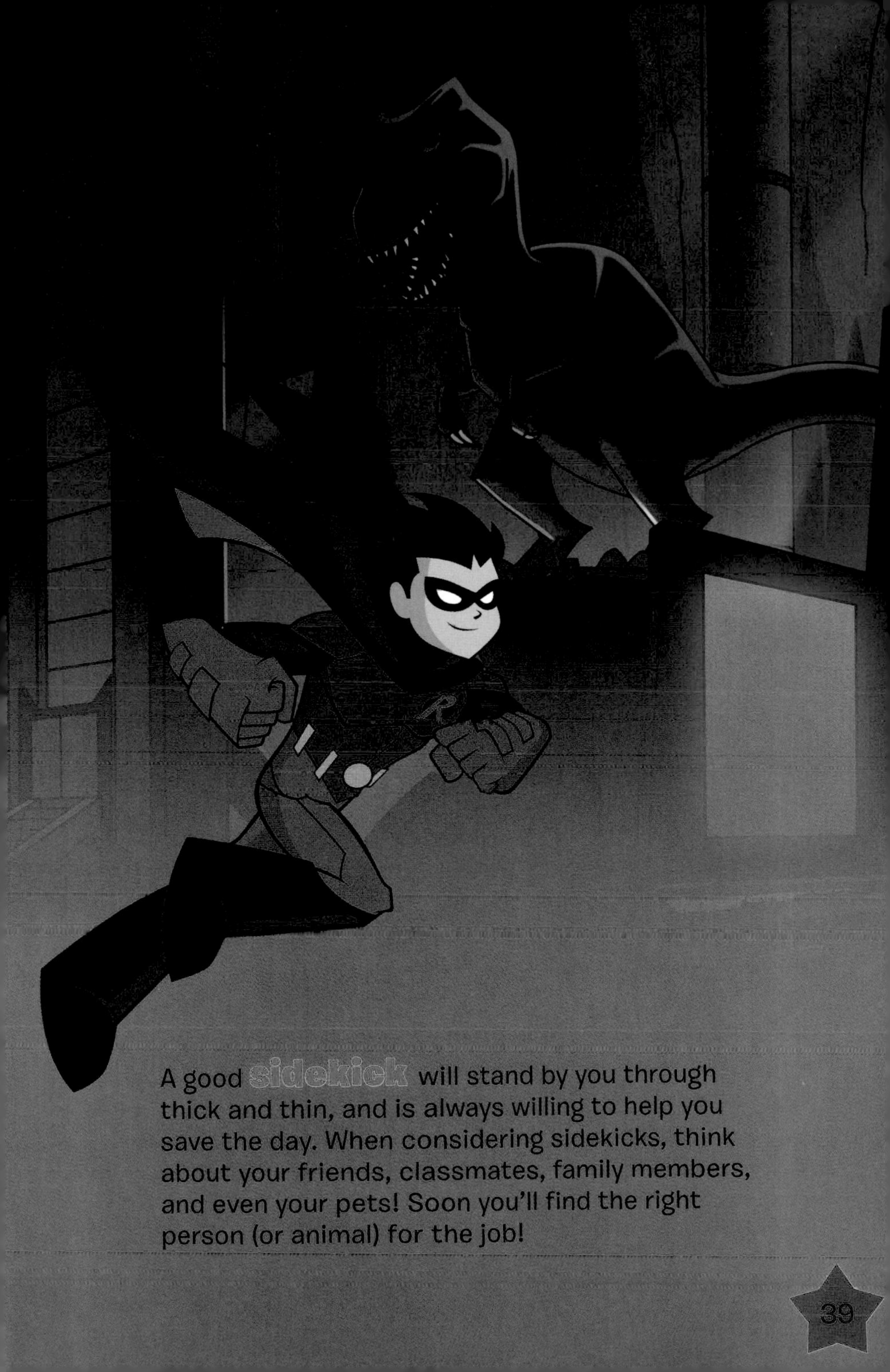

A good **sidekick** will stand by you through thick and thin, and is always willing to help you save the day. When considering sidekicks, think about your friends, classmates, family members, and even your pets! Soon you'll find the right person (or animal) for the job!

Your Headquarters

Every super hero needs a headquarters where he or she can hide out, make plans, and relax. Sometimes this place is secret, like Batman's underground Batcave. Other times, it's in a hard-to-reach place, like Superman's Fortress of Solitude. Whatever you decide, make sure it meets the following criteria:

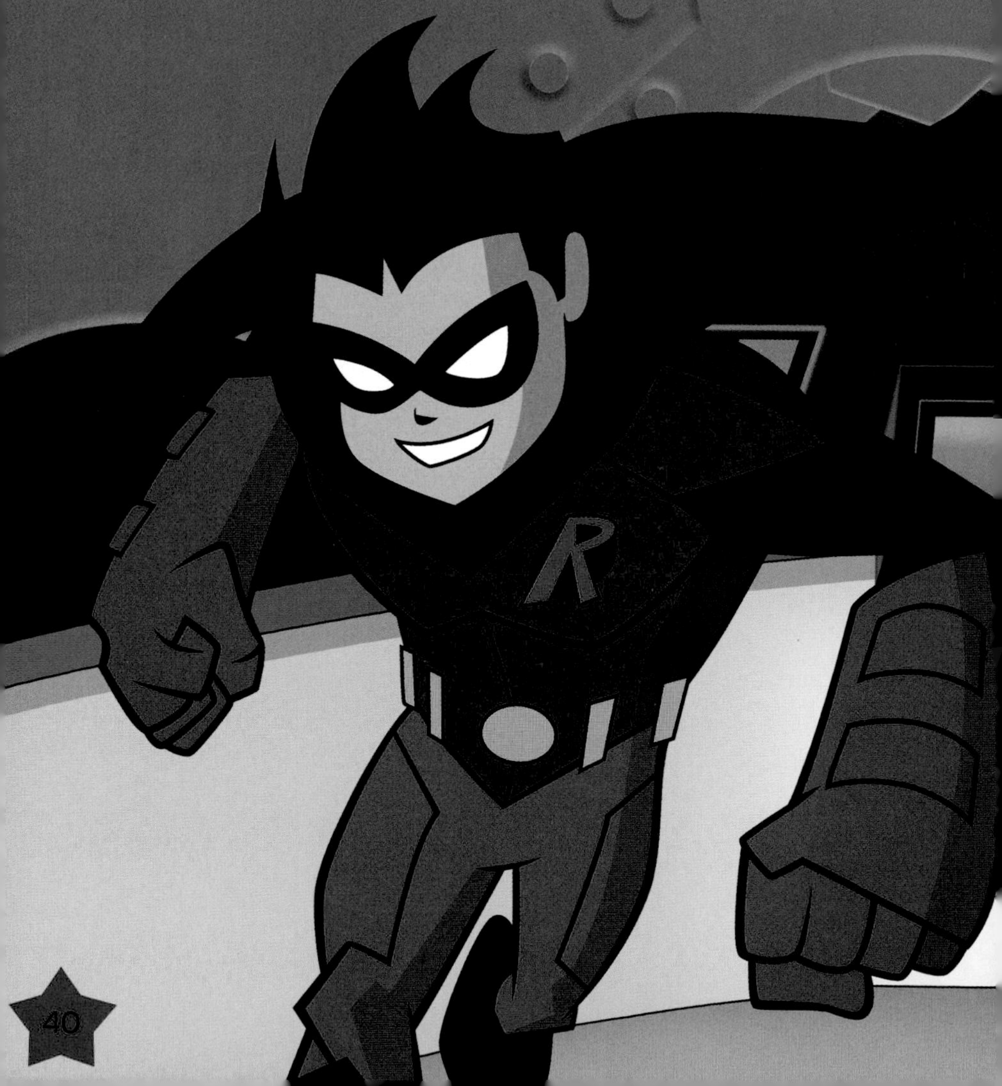

- **It's comfortable:** It should be somewhere that you want to hang out.
- **It's accessible:** Make sure it's easy to get to at a moment's notice.
- **It's safe and secure:** You'll want to make sure that no one—especially villains—touches your super stuff.

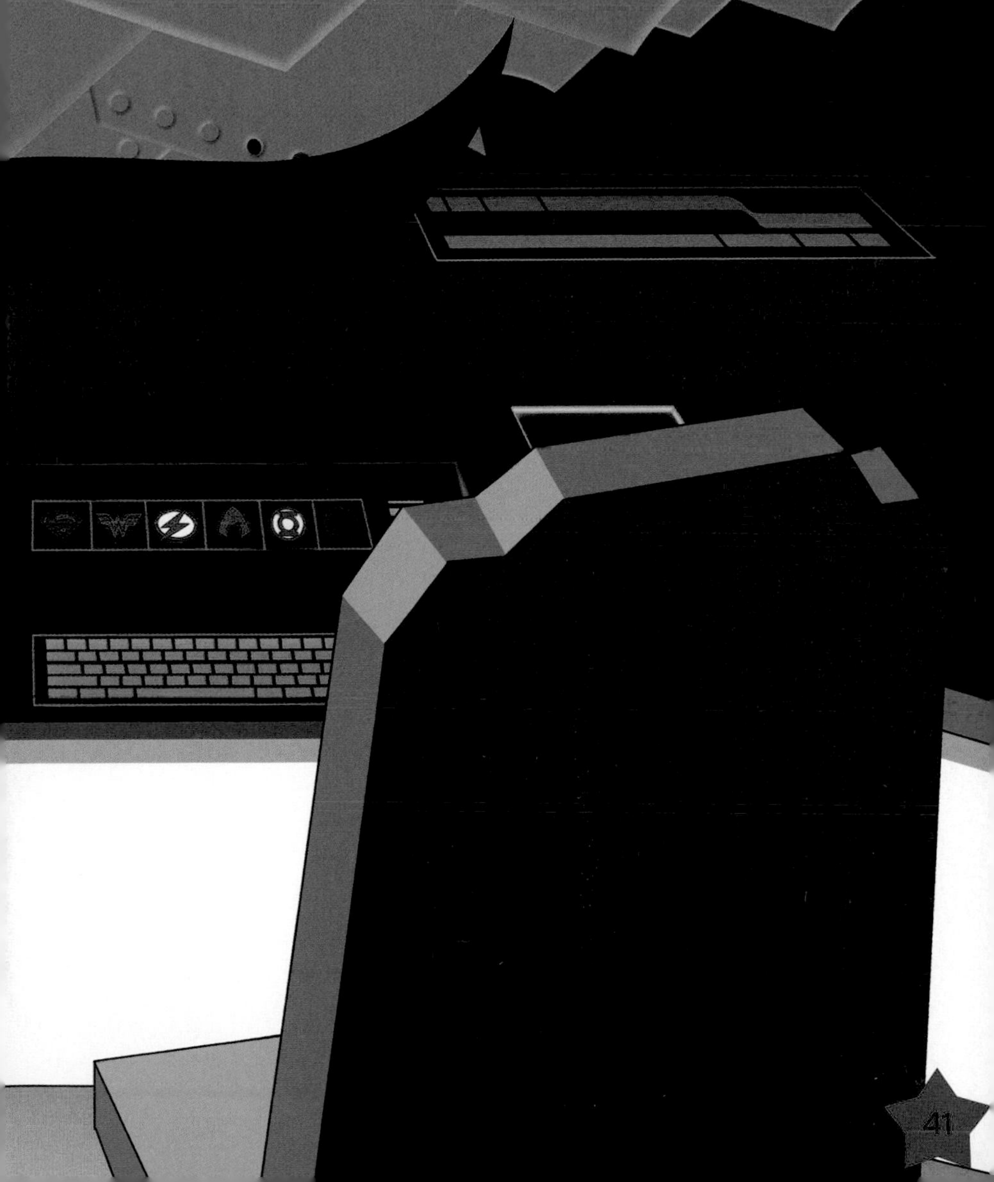

To the Rescue!

Super heroes need to be able to get to the scene of a crime as quickly as possible. If you can run really fast like The Flash or soar through the sky like Superman and Hawkgirl, this is easy! But if you're like the rest of us, you'll need a special mode of transportation.

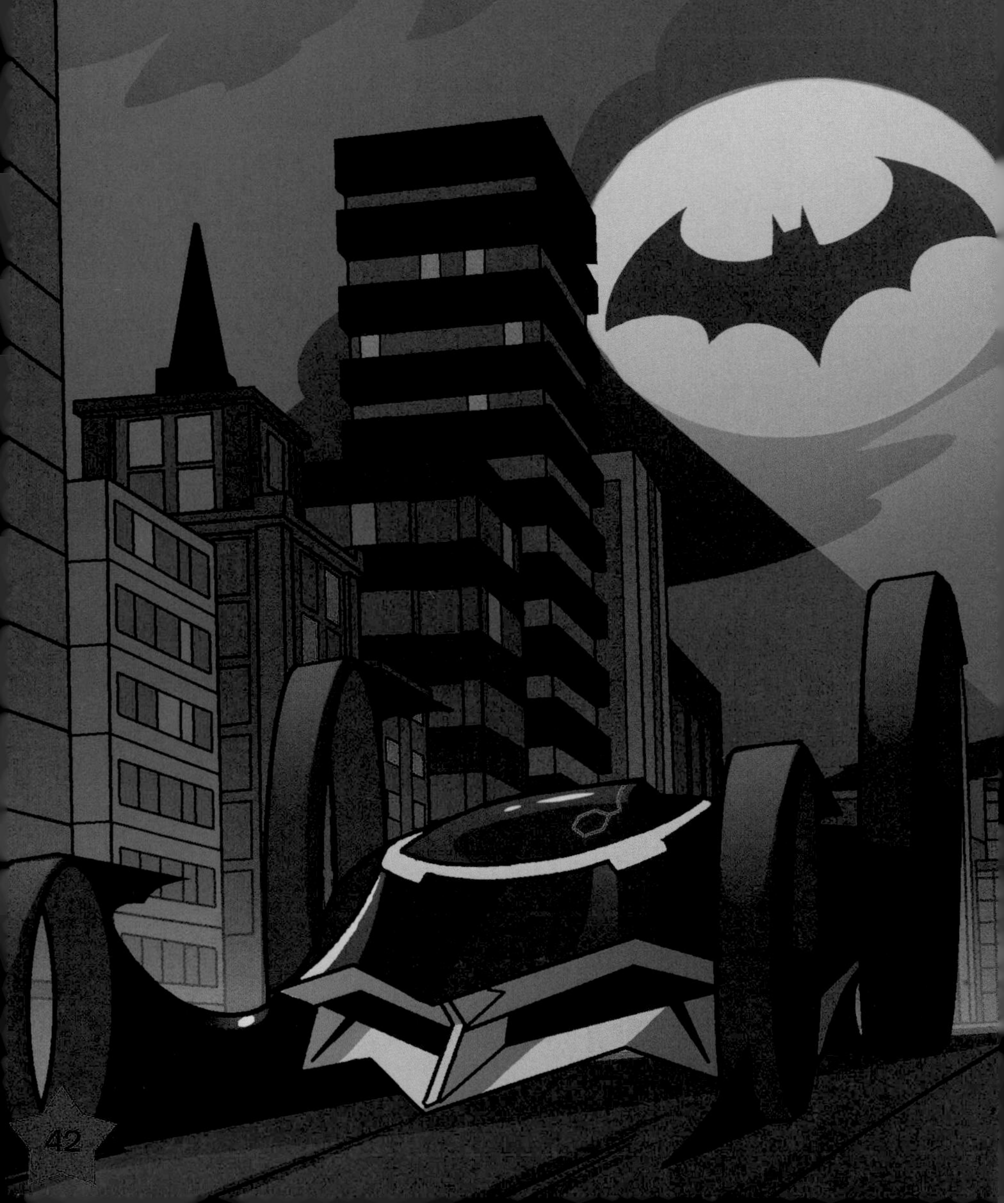

Here are some examples of transport options:

- A motorcycle can get in and out of tight spaces in a jiffy.
- The Batmobile is a mobile crime lab with a powerful computer.
- A stealth jet keeps Wonder Woman hidden from view high in the sky.

Think about your options. Should you use a dirt bike? Inline skates? A skateboard? Decide what works best for you!

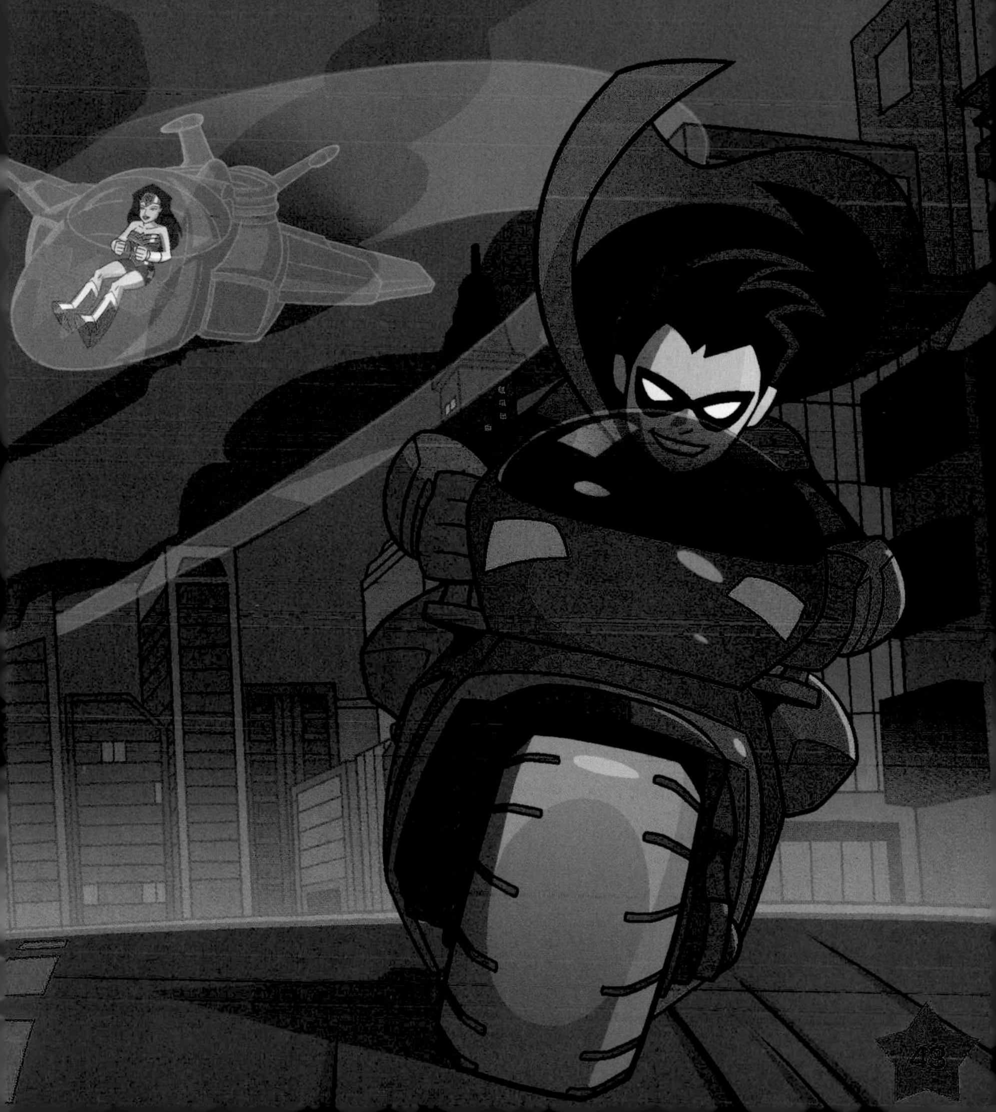

Believe in Yourself

The most important thing about being a hero is believing in yourself! The Super Friends and real-life heroes, like firefighters, work hard to train their minds and bodies and to master necessary skills. There is no easy path to success. But you can reach your full potential by always doing your best and never giving up on your dreams.

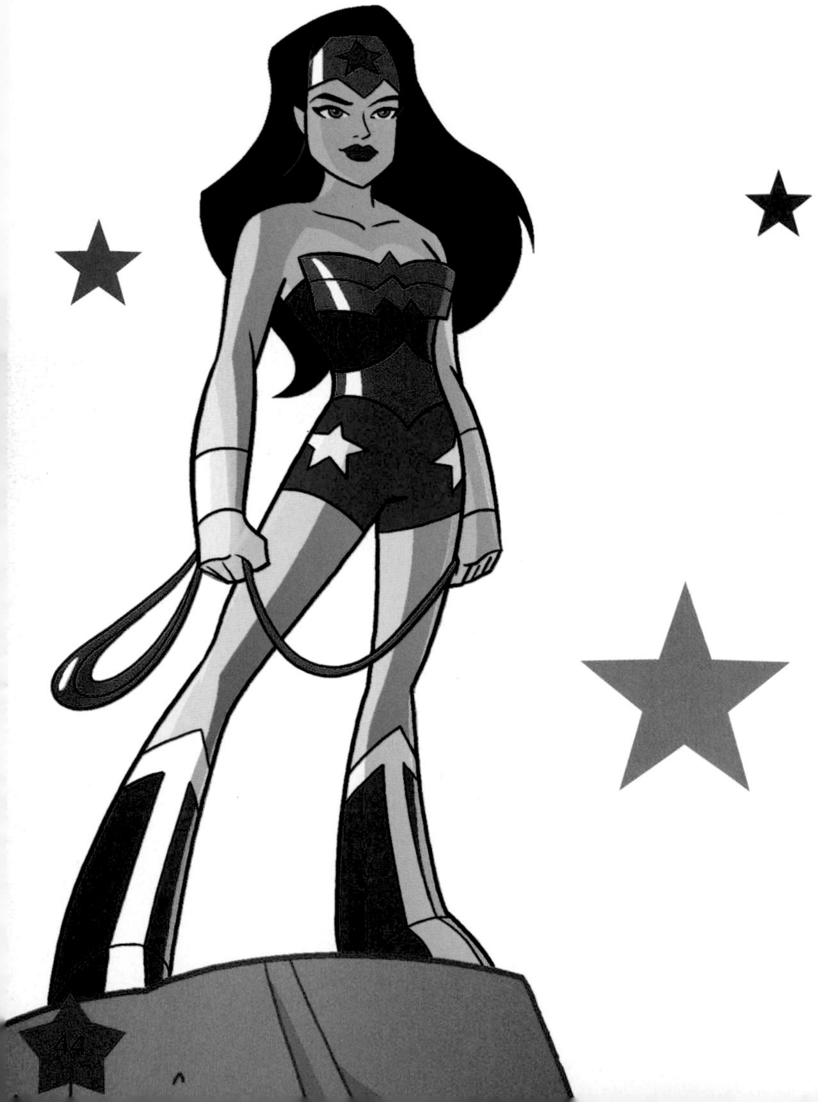

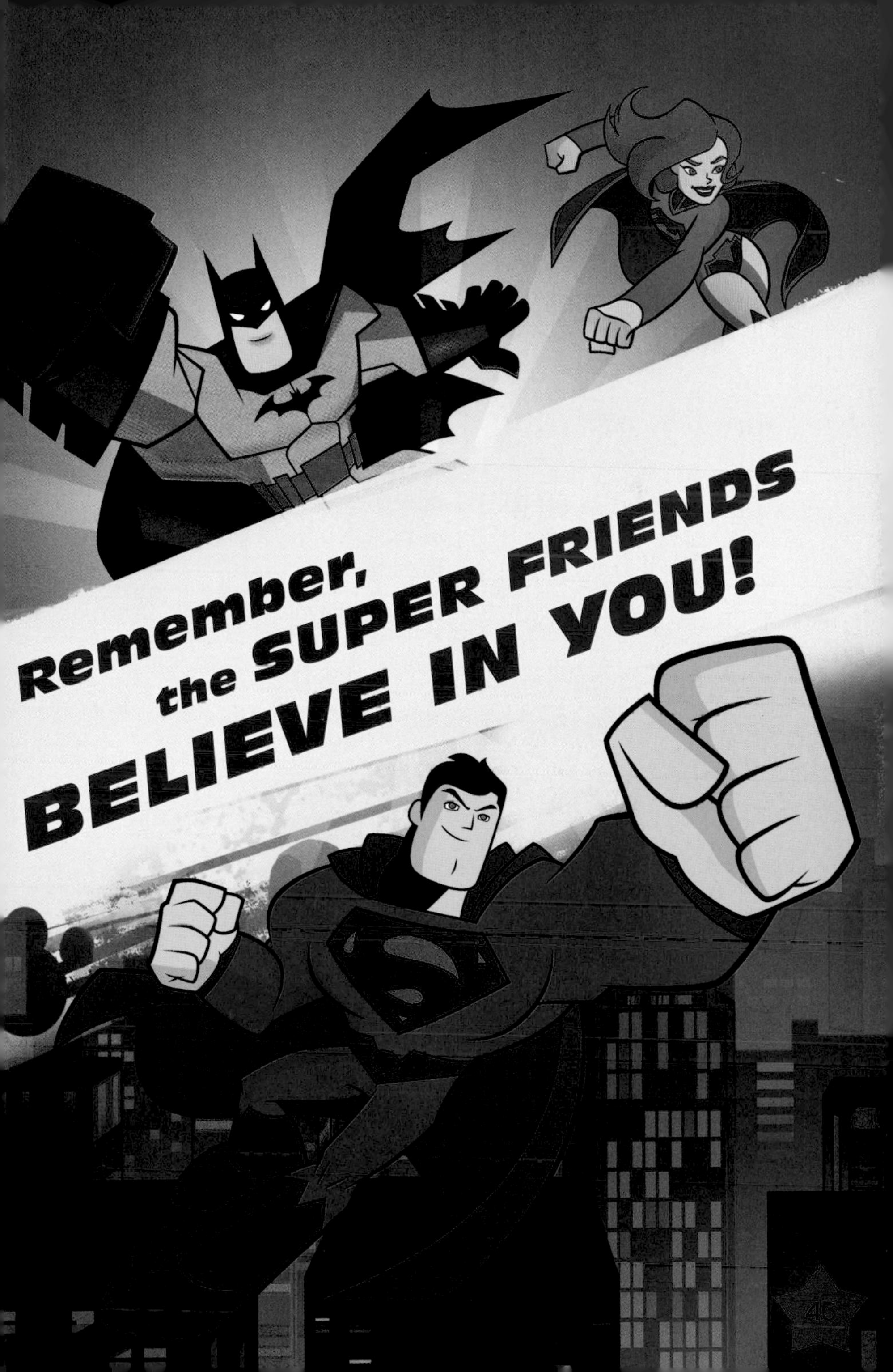
Remember,
the SUPER FRIENDS
BELIEVE IN YOU!

Your Mission

Now that you know exactly what kind of super hero you want to be, you're ready to think about your mission. Choosing a mission is exciting because it is the first step to making a difference in the world. There are lots of things you can do to be a hero right where you are.

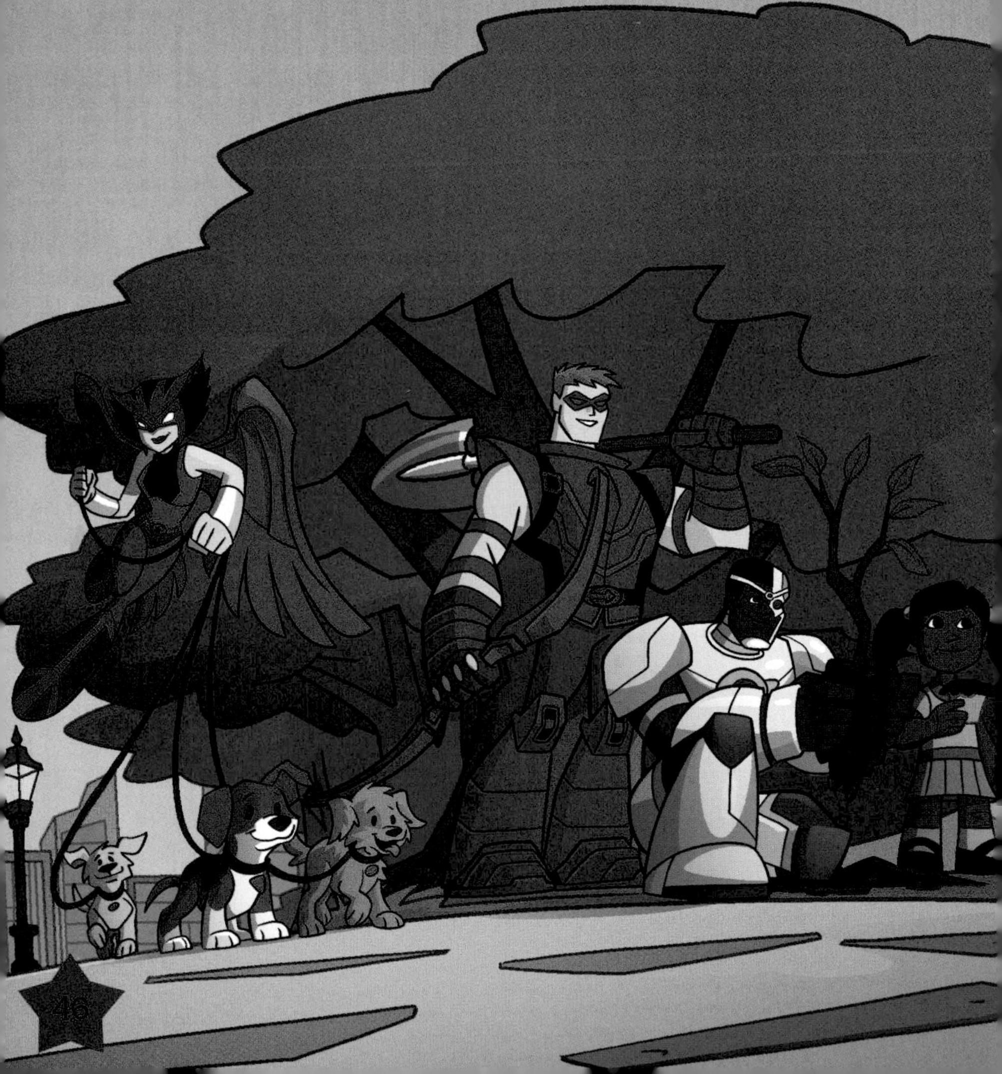

- Help someone with household chores or yard work.
- Help plant trees or flowers in a local park.
- Serve meals to those in need at a local food pantry.
- Speak out against bullying.
- Organize a bake sale or lemonade stand to raise money for a cause that matters to you.
- Volunteer to take care of animals at a nearby animal rescue shelter.
- Read to a sick friend or loved one.

Remember, you don't always have to be moving mountains to make a difference. Even a kind word or a smile is a super way to brighten someone's day!

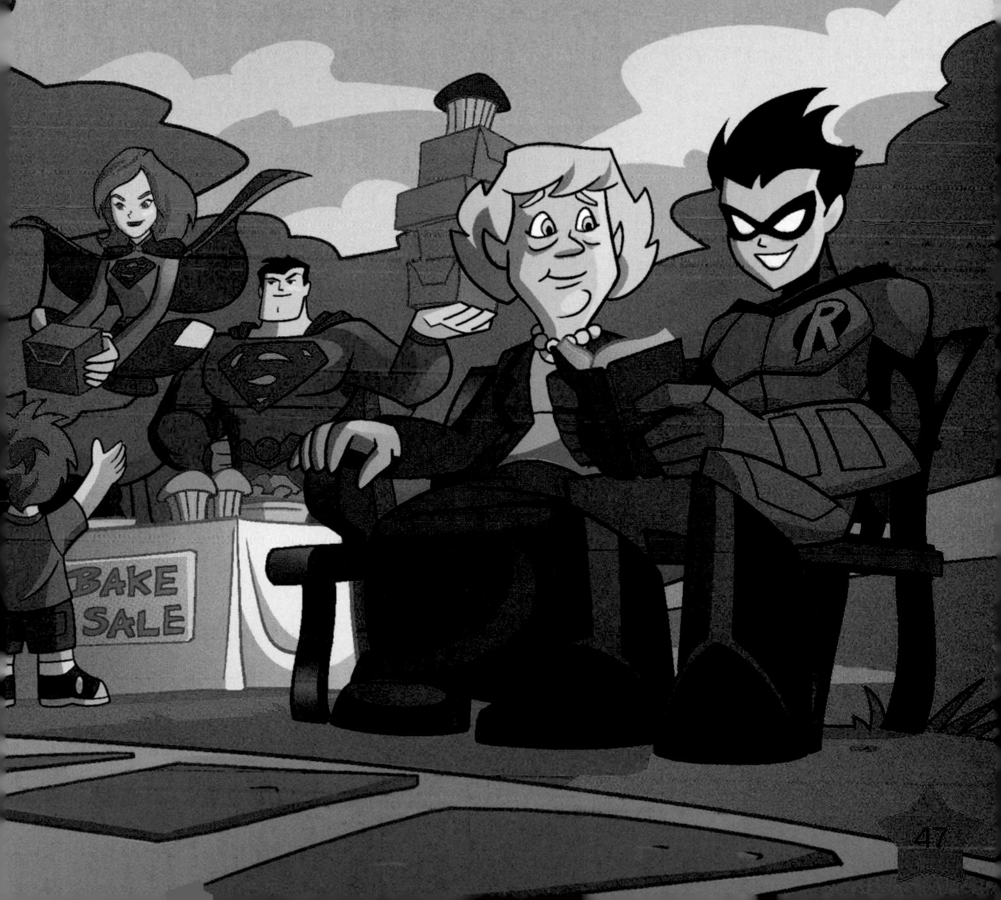
BAKE SALE
R

Hero Practice

Here's an activity to help you build a strong mind and the heart of a hero!

1. Close your eyes and point to a word on the next page.
2. Open your eyes and look at the word you have randomly chosen.
3. Think about what that word means to you.
4. Try to act out your word for the rest of the day.
5. Repeat this process as often as you'd like.

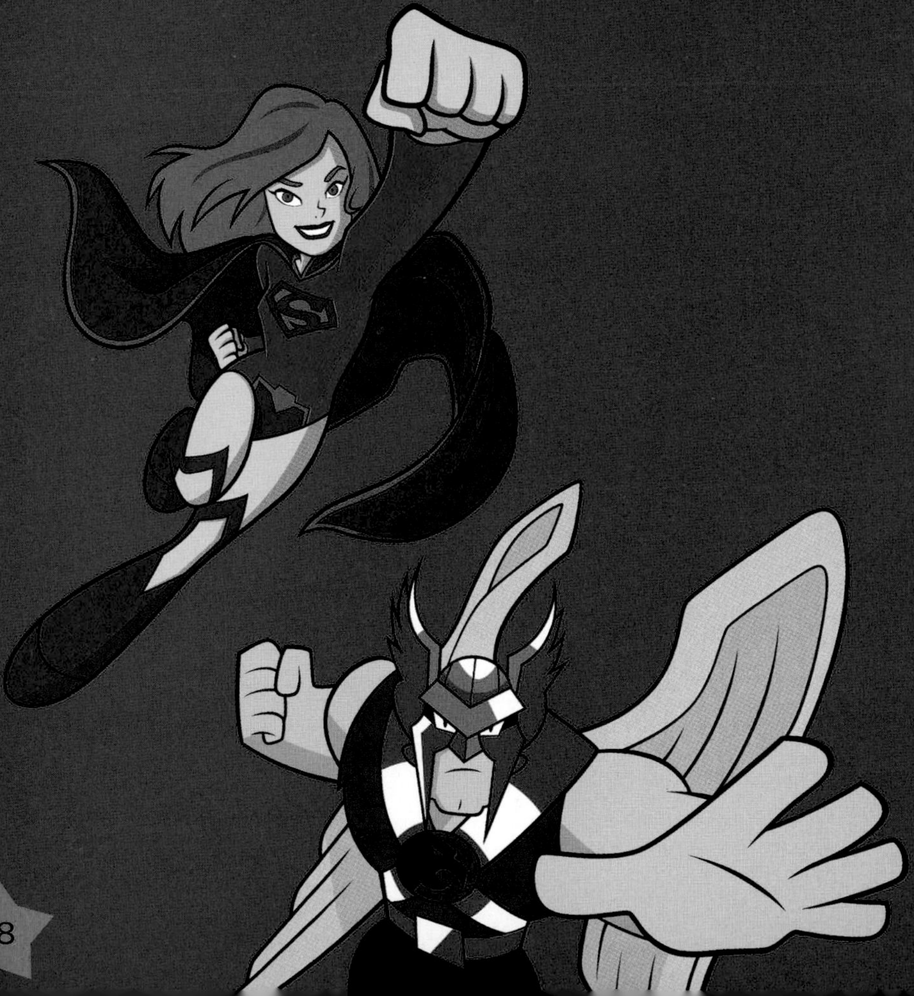

Kind Strong Loyal

Brave Cheerful

Grateful PATIENT

CREATIVE Active

Cooperative

Sincere

 Fair Enthusiastic

Friendly Generous

Hardworking Polite

Independent

Curious Thoughtful

HELPFUL

49

DC SUPER FRIENDS™

HERO
CERTIFICATION
CONGRATULATIONS! YOU'RE A SUPER HERO!

AWARDED TO:

_____

BAD GUYS
AND VILLAINS
— **WARNING** —

**Contents highly dangerous!
For would-be villains only.**

*Super heroes –
Stay out!!!*

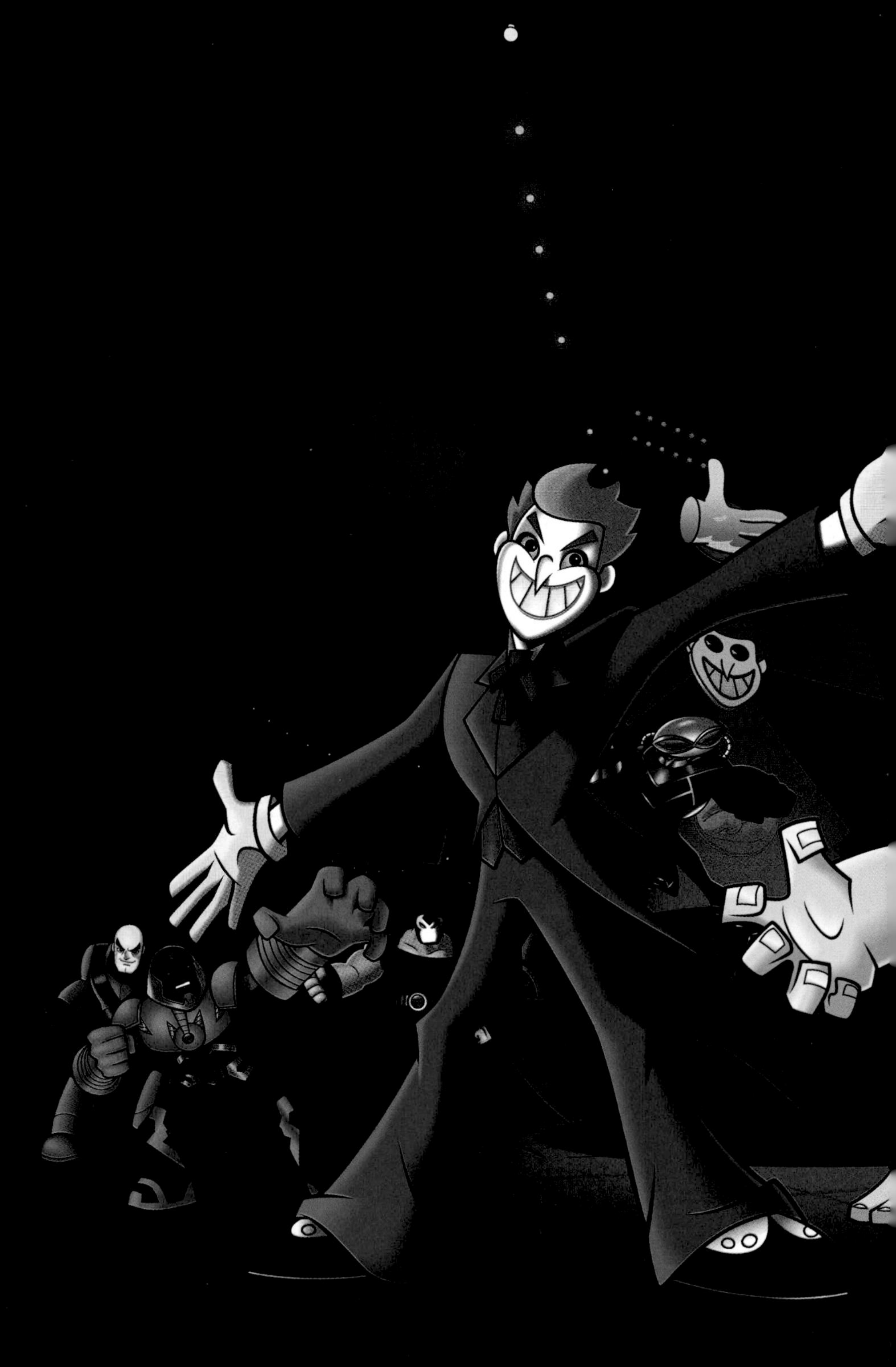

The DC Super-Villains!

The Hero Alternative

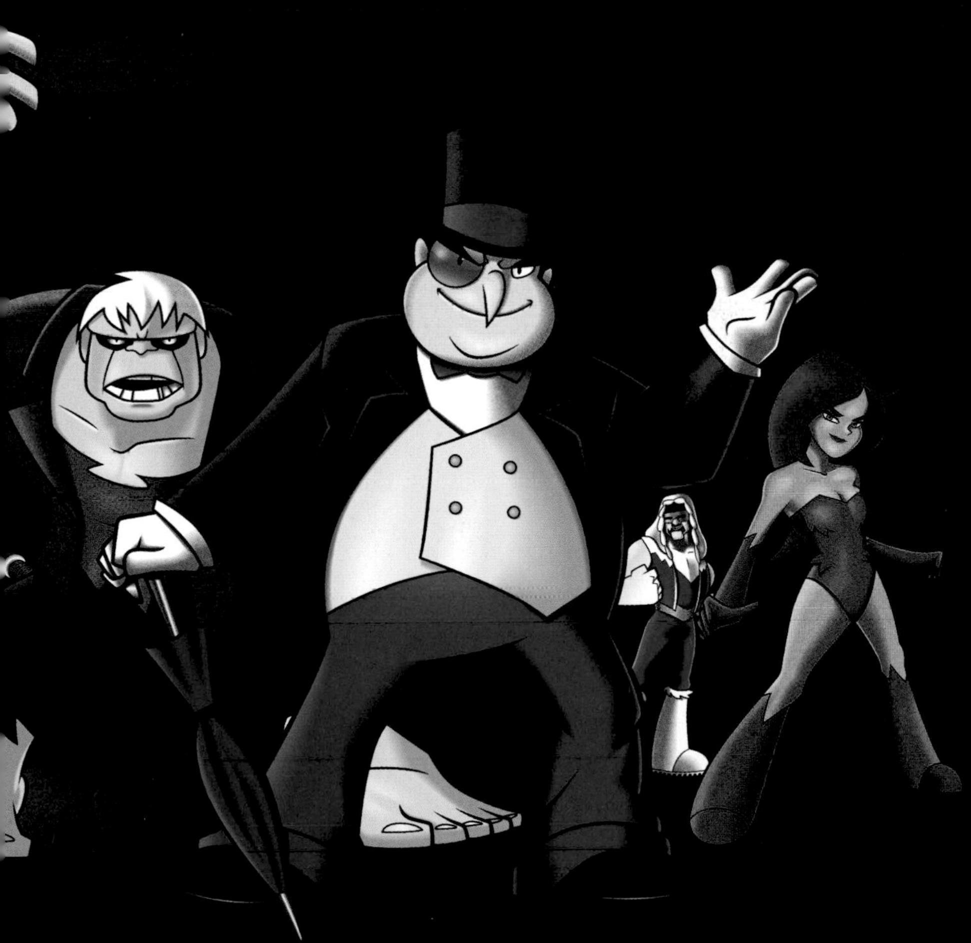

A Life of Crime

Not everyone is cut out to be a super hero. That doesn't mean you have to stand on the sidelines, destined to live a boring, ho-hum life. There is another option—become a super-villain! This super-villain pamphlet contains everything you need to know to be your very worst self!

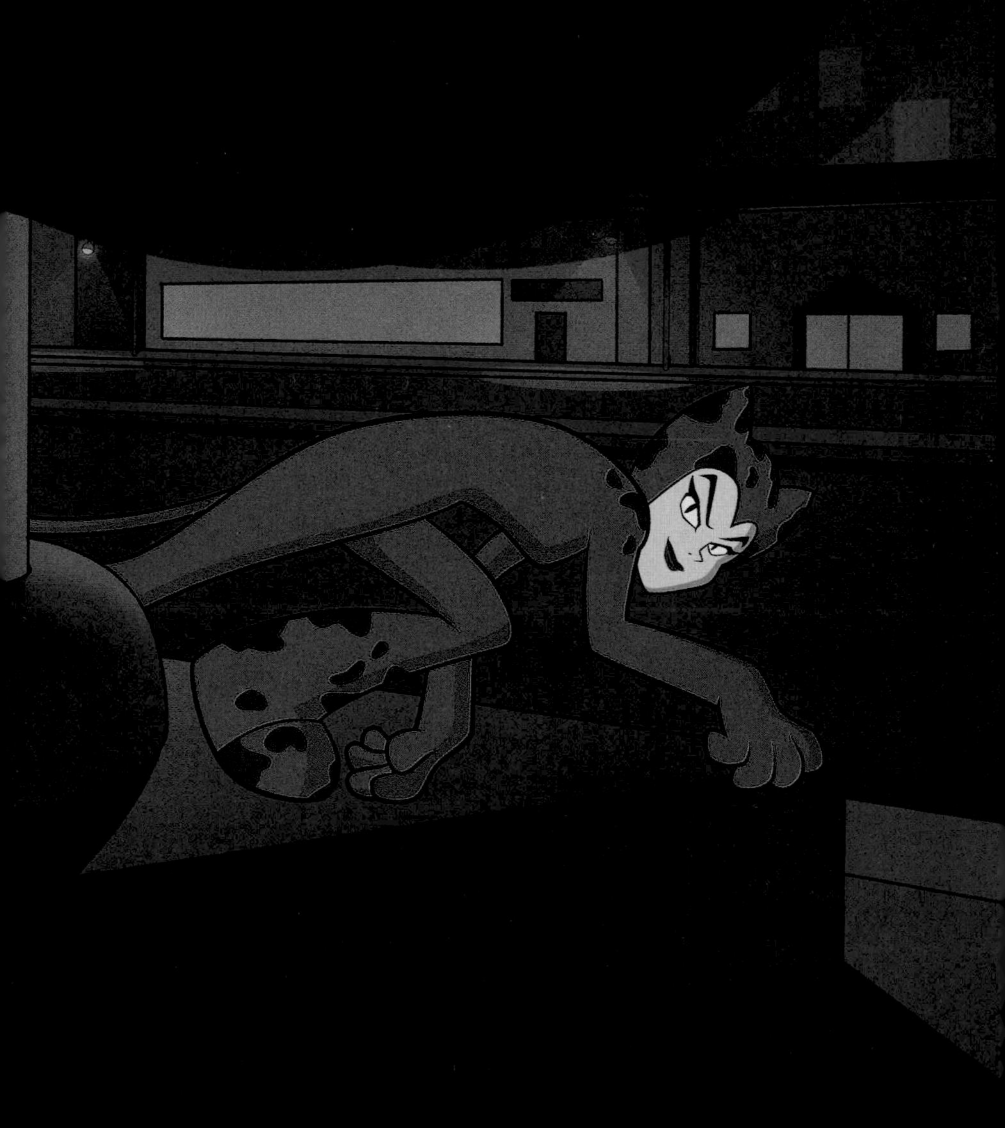

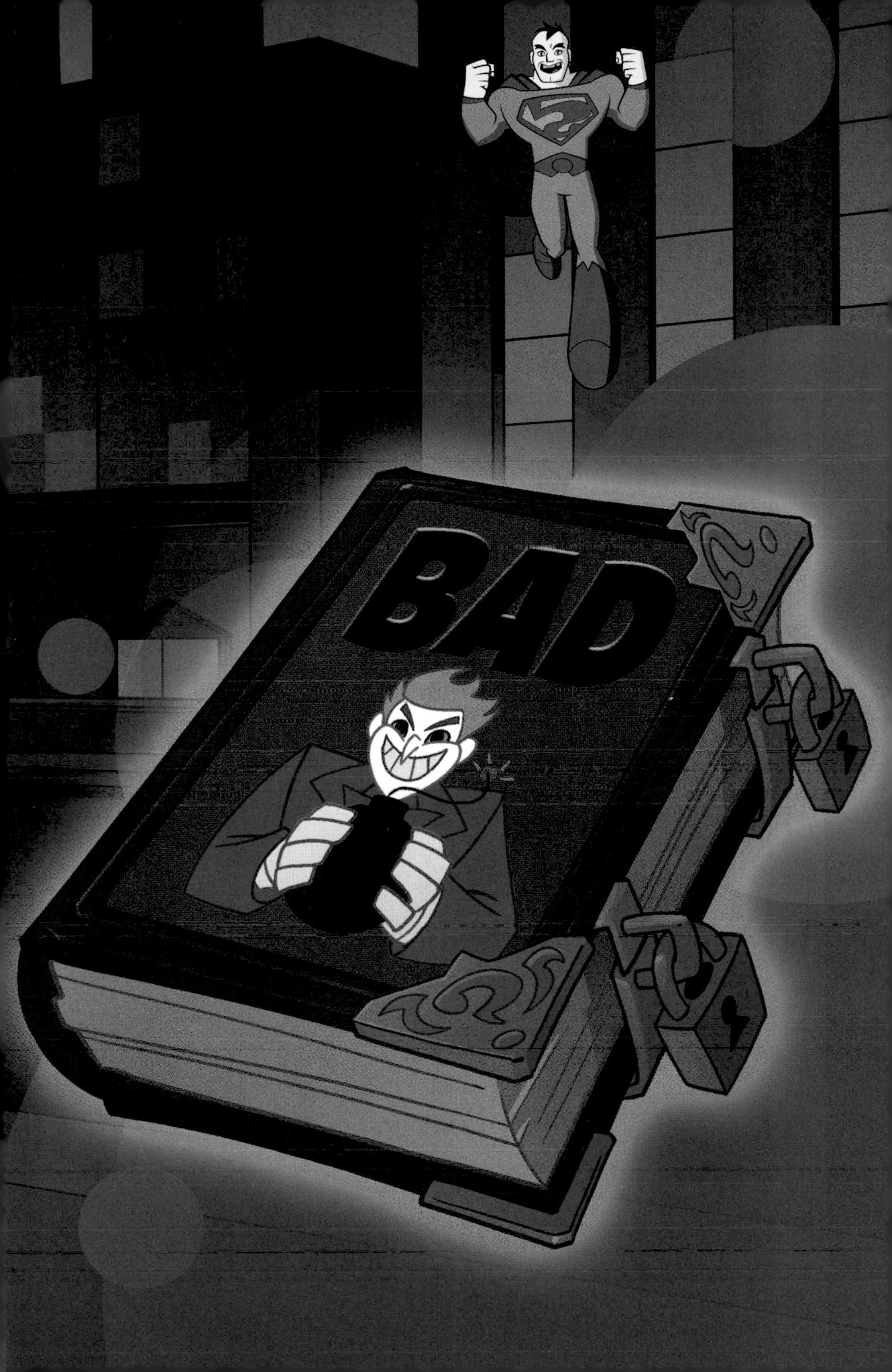
BAD

Why Be Bad?

First of all, forget all that other stuff you read earlier. You don't need it. Helping others? Saving the day? Nonsense. Instead, try helping yourself and ruining someone's day! It's much more fun, and in the end, isn't that what being a super-villain is all about?

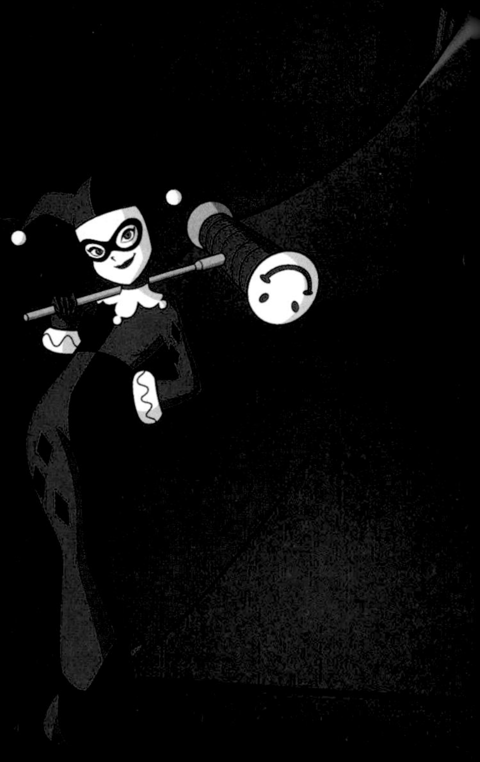

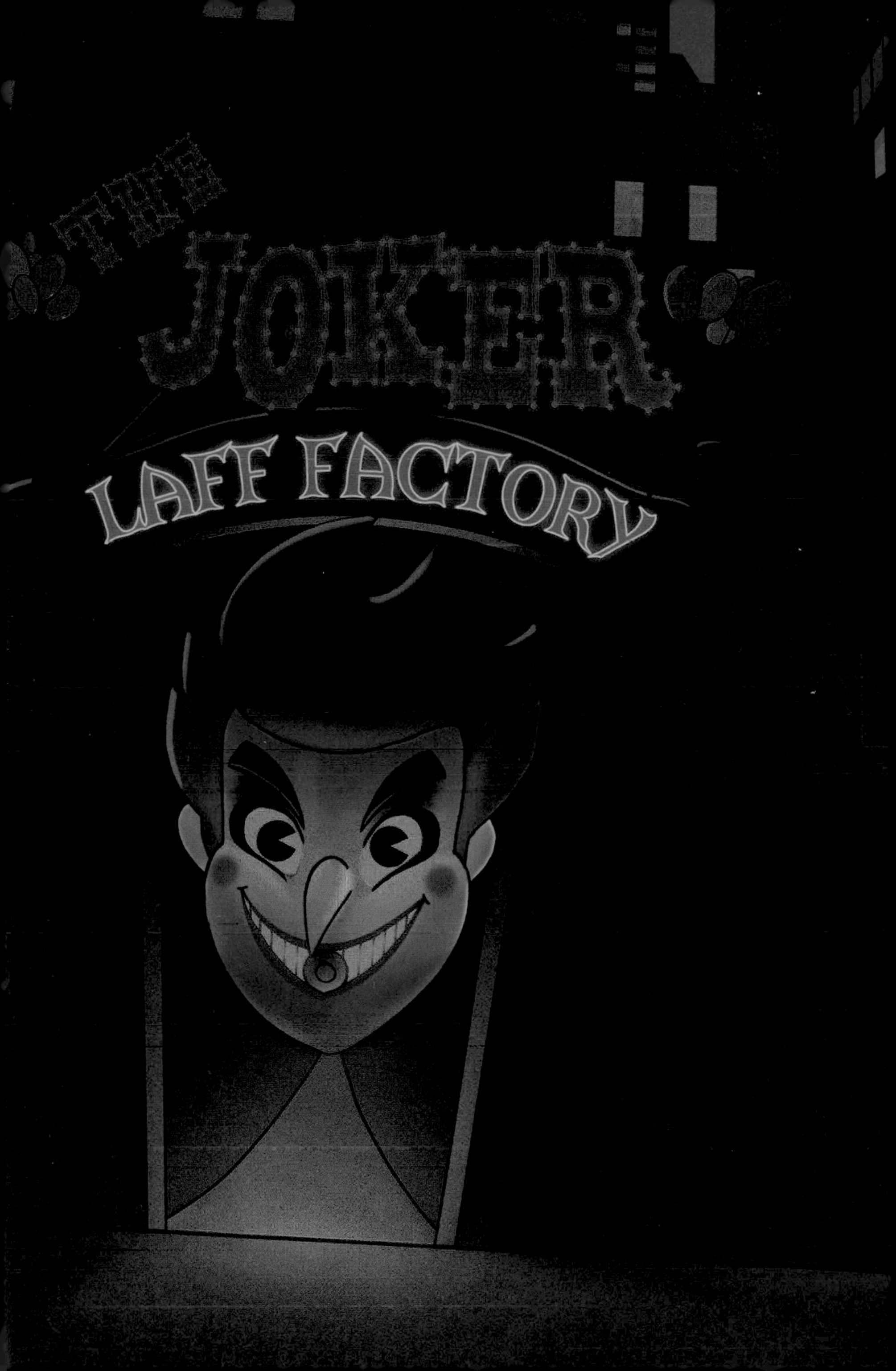
THE
JOKER
LAFF FACTORY

Choosing a Villainous Persona

There is no one-size-fits-all option when it comes to villainy. You have to find the persona that fits your evil intentions. Check out this list of DC super-villains for some ideas. They are good examples of being bad!

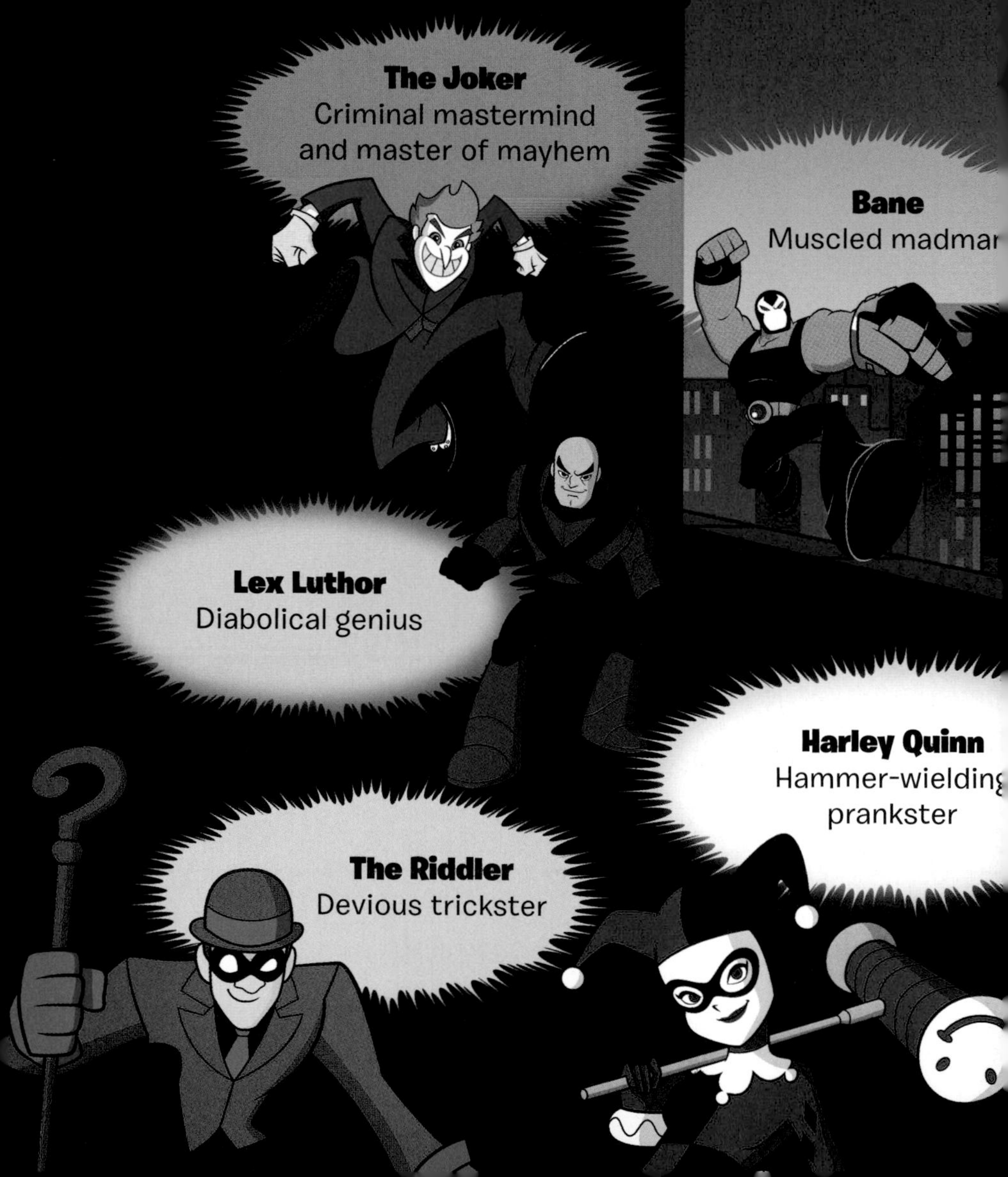

The Joker
Criminal mastermind and master of mayhem
Bane
Muscled madma
Lex Luthor
Diabolical genius
Harley Quinn
Hammer-wieldin
prankster
The Riddler
Devious trickster

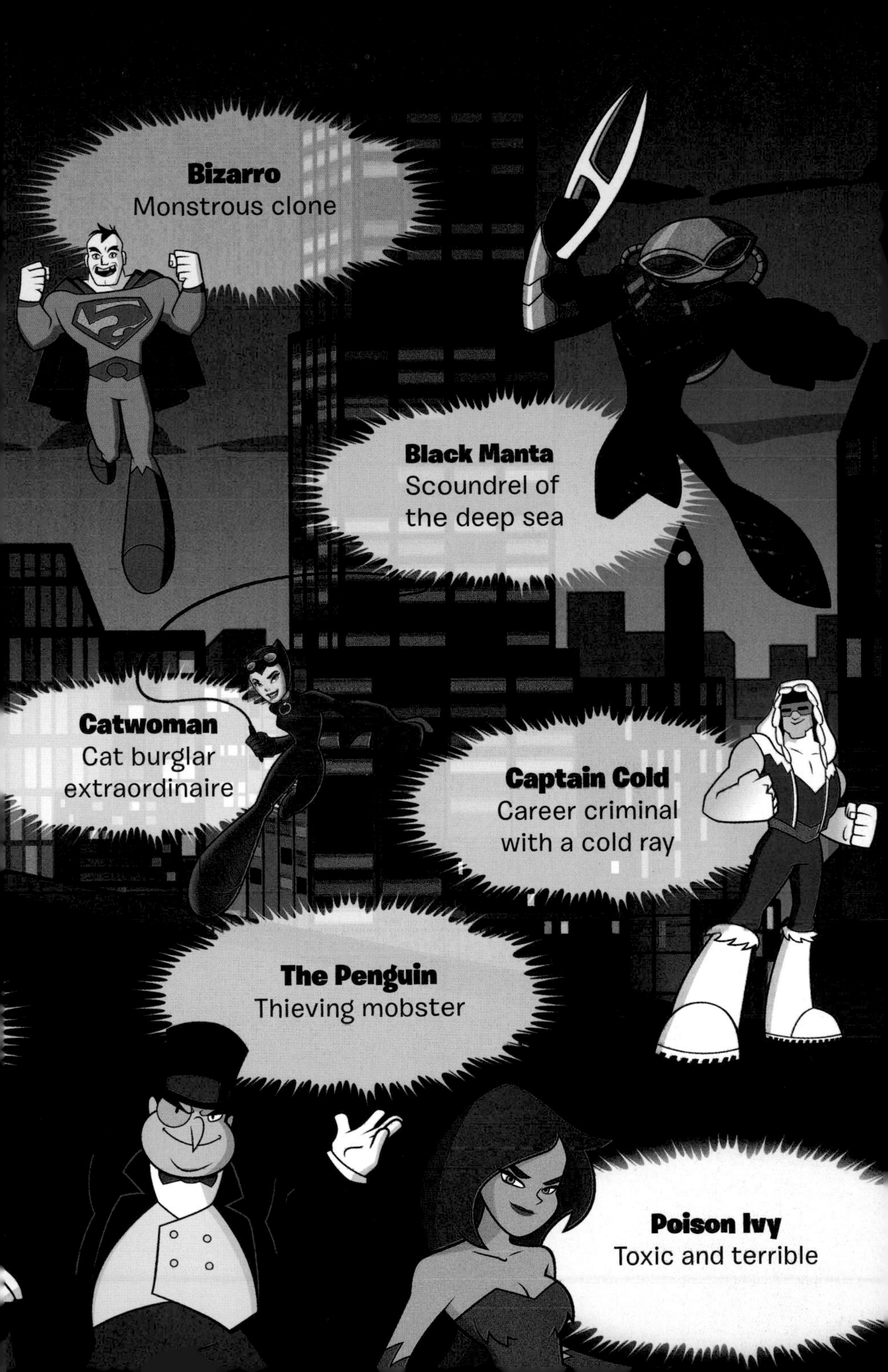
Bizarro
Monstrous clone
Black Manta
Scoundrel of the deep sea
Catwoman
Cat burglar extraordinaire
Captain Cold
Career criminal with a cold ray
The Penguin
Thieving mobster
Poison Ivy
Toxic and terrible

Membership Test for the Legion of Doom

You find a wallet on the ground. What do you do?

A. Return it to its owner yourself.

B. Take it to the closest police department.

C. Snoop through its contents.

D. Take everything in it and throw it on the ground next to a perfectly good trash can!

You pass a jewelry store. What do you do?

A. Buy a gift for a friend.

B. Admire the jewels from afar.

C. Pocket a couple of pearls when no one is looking.

D. Smash the cases and grab everything you can get your hands on!

You pass an art museum. What do you do?

A. Make a donation.

B. Take a tour of the new exhibit.

C. Add smiley faces to some paintings.

D. Steal priceless works of art in a massive heist!

You see a bank. What do you do?

A. Deposit a check.

B. Ask for a free lollipop.

C. Steal the pen on the counter.

D. Break into the vault and let money rain down around you!

Look at the letter choice you selected most often. If you answered mostly A to these questions, you probably don't have what it takes to be a super-villain. Same thing if you answered mostly B. If you answered C, you have potential, but you still need some work. If you answered mostly D, the Legion of Doom has a place for you!

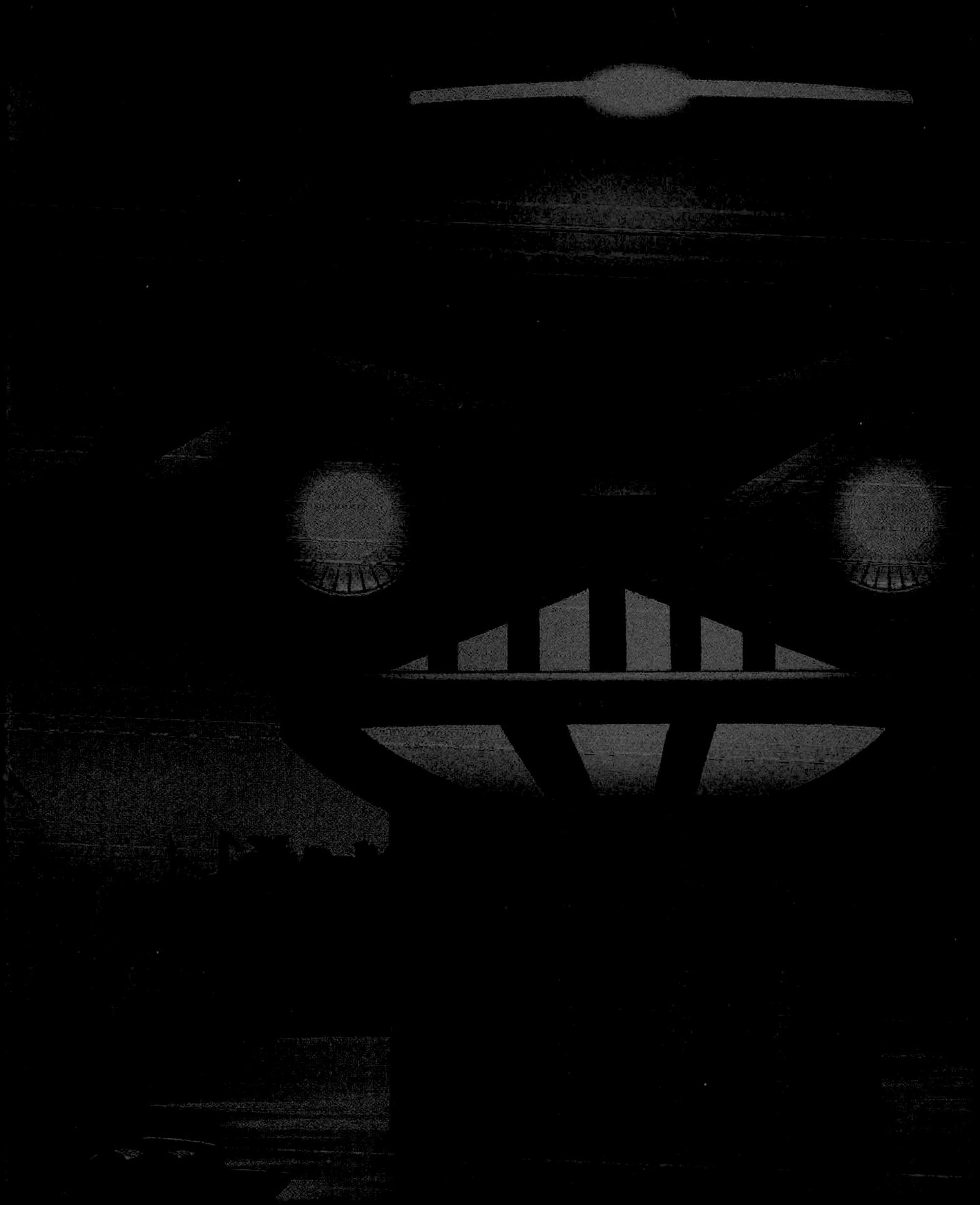

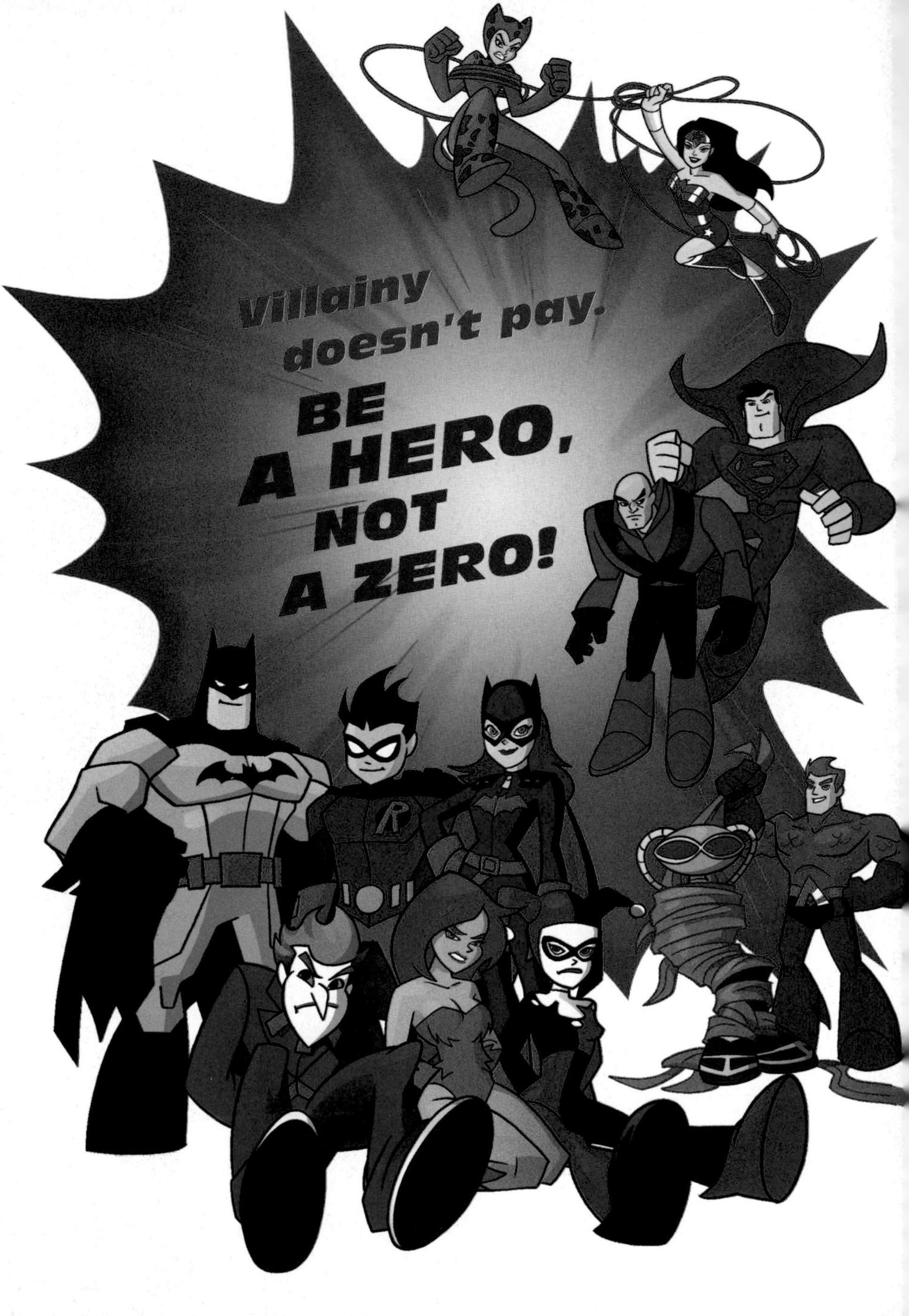
Villainy
doesn't pay.
BE
A HERO,
NOT
A ZERO!

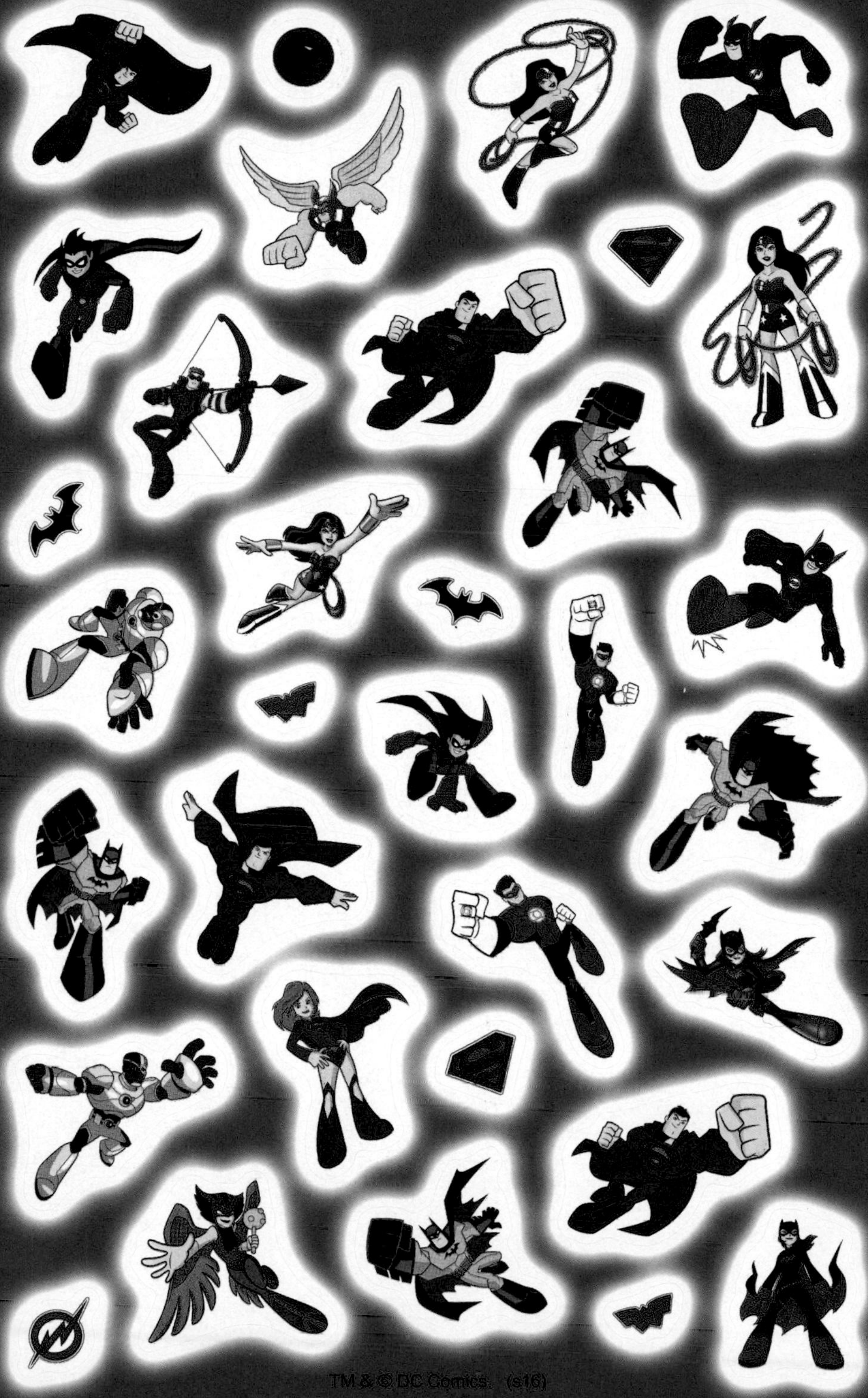

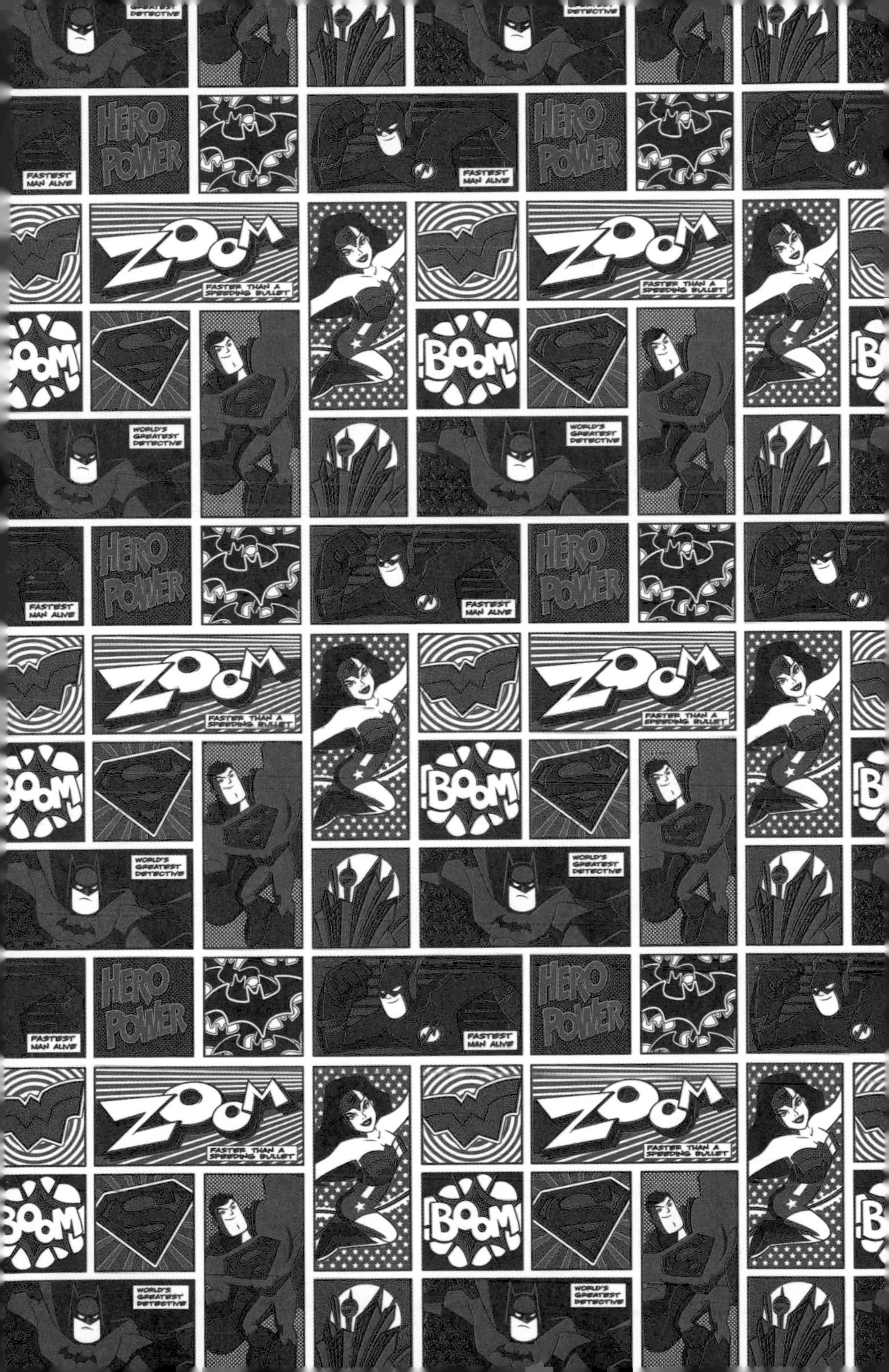
HERO POWER
FASTEST MAN ALIVE
ZOOM
FASTER THAN A SPEEDING BULLET
BOOM!
WORLD'S GREATEST DETECTIVE

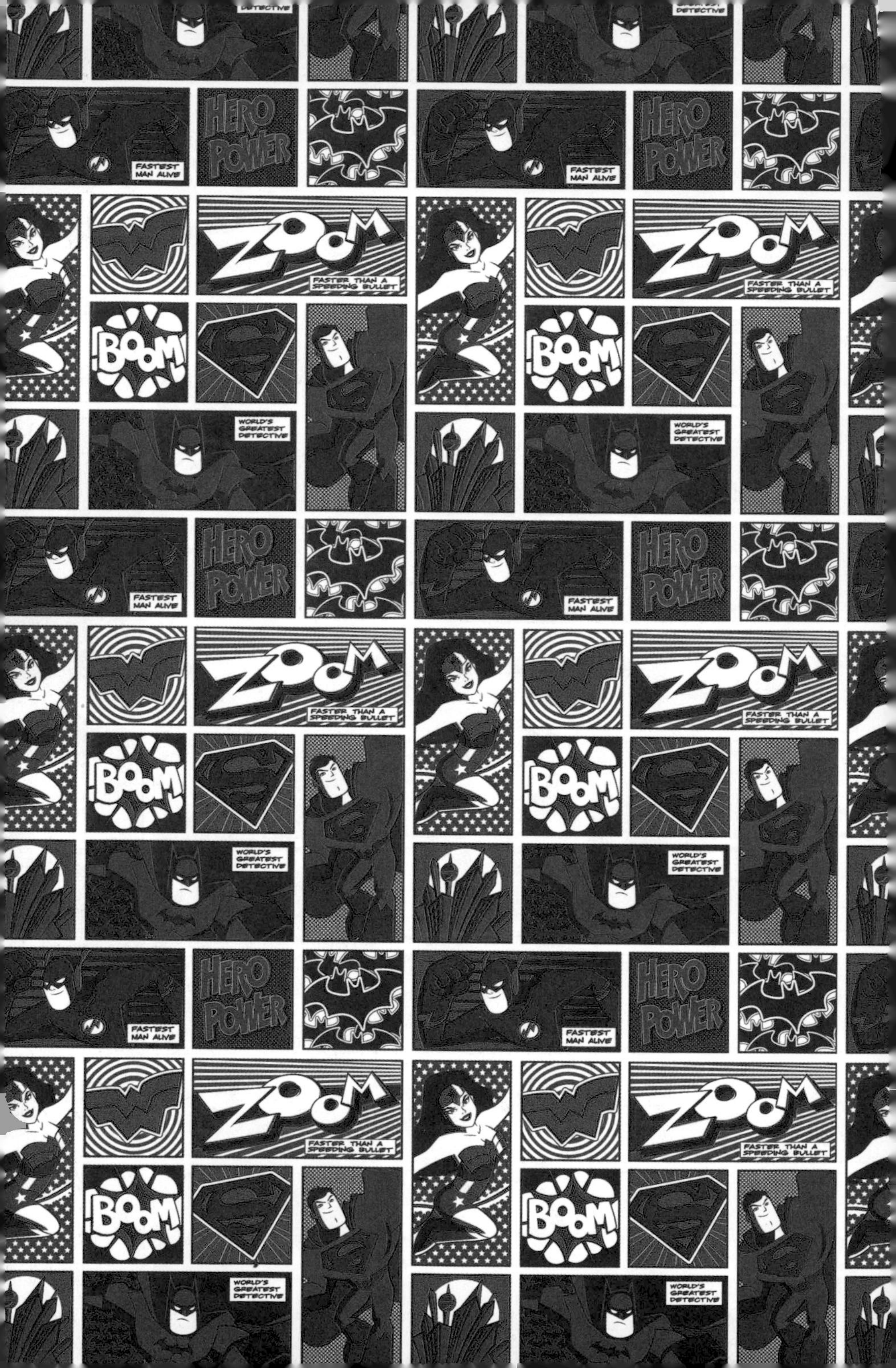
HERO POWER
FASTEST MAN ALIVE
ZOOM
FASTER THAN A SPEEDING BULLET
BOOM!
WORLD'S GREATEST DETECTIVE